10-7

10-7

X-INDIAN CHRONICLES

X-INDIAN CHRONICLES

The Book of Mausape

THOMAS M. YEAHPAU

CANDLEWICK PRESS
CAMBRIDGE, MASSACHUSETTS

First edition 2006

Library of Congress Cataloging-in-Publication Data

Yeahpau, Thomas M.
X-Indian chronicles : the book of Mausape / Thomas M. Yeahpau. —1st ed.
p.   cm.
Summary: A collection of interwoven stories that chronicles the lives of several X-Indians—those Indians who have lost their traditional beliefs, traditions, and medicines—as they grow up and become young men.
ISBN-13: 978-0-7636-2706-5
ISBN-10: 0-7636-2706-2
1. Indians of North America—Juvenile fiction. 2. Children's stories, American.
[1. Indians of North America—Fiction. 2. Conduct of life—Fiction.
3. Short Stories.] I. Title.
PZ7.Y323Xi   2006
[Fic]—dc22   2006042575

2 4 6 8 10 9 7 5 3 1

Printed in the United States of America

This book was typeset in M Bembo.

Candlewick Press
2067 Massachusetts Avenue
Cambridge, Massachusetts 02140

visit us at www.candlewick.com

THIS BOOK IS DEDICATED

TO ALL MY NATIVES,

BUT ESPECIALLY

DEDICATED

TO

RODERICK BERT

A. J. WHITEBULL

RICHARD TARTSAH

JOSEPH ALBIN BERT

MICHAEL "REDDOG" REDELK

AND

TO EVERY POOR INDIAN KID

WHO DARES TO DREAM

WHERE DREAMS ARE

RARELY DREAMT.

PART I

An X-Indian Legend

The X-Indians were born
of circuitry, of mechanisms
They were born in a world
inside of a world
filled with stories
filled with tradition
filled with formulas
filled with visions
But they were trapped inside
of this world inside of a world
Until one day, Saynday came along
the trickster saw his people
they were angry
they were glad
they were scared
they were sad
Saynday grabbed his medicine
and blew a hole right in the middle
of that world inside of a world
and he freed his people, every boy, every girl
some girls like Ginger
some girls like Mary Ann
some boys like the Skipper

some boys like Gilligan
But they were all soon marooned on a new island
made of concrete, inside a whole new world
and it was inside the Indian Territory
that the X-Indians began their story

Deer Lady
1985

Mausape Onthaw was an X-Indian. He belonged to a
race that was losing its culture and to a generation that
was losing its mind. His grandpa was an Indian. Indians
still had their traditions, their beliefs, and their medicine.
They had very little of the white man's ways. It was assimilation that ultimately kept the Indians and X-Indians
from belonging to the same race. They were alike in some
ways, but they were also different in many others.

Mausape idolized his grandpa, even though his grandpa
had rarely been around for most of his life. Over the years
there had been postcards from far-off places, even different countries. For an old Indian man, his grandpa sure got
around a lot. He was always on the road, never staying in
one place for any length of time. Only on his way through

the Indian Territory would he stop and visit Mausape's grandma and Mausape. No one ever knew why he traveled so much, but then again, no one had the audacity to ask a medicine man his business. So a mystery it remained.

One day, Mausape and his grandma received one of them rare visits from his grandpa, who seemed more tired than usual. And he didn't look too healthy, either. It looked as if the days on the road and nights in hotel rooms were catching up with him. Still, he swore everything was fine and that he just needed some rest. And rest he did. For three days he stayed in his old room, only coming out to eat or use the bathroom.

While his grandpa got his rest, Mausape waited anxiously. He always looked forward to going with his grandpa to do his usual business around NDN City. They would sometimes collect herbs for medicine, find sage for ritual purposes, or just take long walks, during which his grandpa would pass down some of his ancient knowledge.

Finally, the day came when his grandpa emerged from his confinement, his face full of color again and a perfect smile placed across it.

"Let's go, Kone," his grandpa said before Mausape even had a chance to greet him.

They drove into NDN City to "gather medicine." That was what his grandpa said they had to do first. After eating a nice dinner at the local bowling alley, the two of them bowled a few frames. Mausape had improved since the last time they had "gathered medicine." After that they went to Dairy Queen, and over a banana split, his grandpa told him all about the desert and the Navajos. They were good people, he said.

The sun had set and night had already blanketed the sky by the time they drove out of NDN City and made their way home. It was one of those Indian nights, still and uncertain, with a familiar but distrusting aura in the air. Mausape sat quietly and listened to his grandpa's wise words. He was a living encyclopedia. He knew everything there was to know, even things you couldn't find in books. Mausape wanted to be just like him someday.

His grandpa was telling him about the last Kiowa Sun Dance when they felt a thud and heard a thunderous explosion in front of the truck. His grandpa slammed on the brakes, and they came to a screeching halt.

"Kone! You all right?" his grandpa asked with the deepest concern.

"Yeah, Grandpa," Mausape answered. He had caught himself on the dashboard. "What was that?"

"I hit something. Looked like a deer. I'd better go see. You wait here, Kone."

His grandpa reached into the glove compartment and pulled out a small medicine pouch, then got out of the truck and walked around to the front to see what they had hit. His grandpa found nothing, which relieved Mausape because he hated the thought of killing anything, especially a deer. Yet something on the grille of the truck had caught his grandpa's attention. They *had* hit something. Mausape could see it in his grandpa's eyes, see it in the way his grandpa sprinkled the contents of the medicine pouch around the truck. Mausape watched with a learning eye. He hadn't known there was a ritual for hitting an animal.

When his grandpa finally got back inside the truck, Mausape couldn't help asking what he'd been doing. His grandpa, however, didn't answer him. Something was wrong. The gleaming color that had come back into his grandpa's face after the days of rest was gone. He was pale again. It was only when they were far down the road that he finally spoke.

"Kone, I'm old, and the older I get, the harder it gets for me to run," he said.

"Run?"

"Yes, run. You know, Kone, there's something I've been meaning to tell you for so long. You probably won't understand it now, but someday you will. I owe it to you to tell you why I've been absent for most of your life." Mausape looked at his grandpa, unsure of what to say; so he said nothing. "There are things of this world and things not of this world, Kone. And you have to have a keen eye if you want to see both."

"Keen? What does that mean, Grandpa?"

"It just means strong, powerful. I'm going to tell you a story, Kone, and I want you to listen carefully."

"With keen ears?"

"Yes, with keen ears, Kone," his grandpa said with a smile. Then he told this story:

"A long, long time ago, Kone, when I was just a young man, I was what a lot of people called pow-wow born. That just meant that if there was a pow-wow going on, I was there. I had it in my blood. But this was also around the time I was learning the ways of the earth, medicine, so it was more of an obligation for me to be at every pow-wow. Those were the good ole days, when pow-wows were pow-wows. Anyhoo, there was this decent-size one that they always used to have up in the Massacre Hills. They don't have it anymore, but it was a good one. I went to it every year. Well, one year, right after your father was born, I ended up going to it with some of my friends. Your dad had gotten sick and your grandma had to stay home with him. She never liked pow-wows all that much, anyway.

"And that night, it was big. I mean, everybody in the I.T. was there. You could see heads as far as the bonfire allowed you to. You see, back then dancers used to dance around a fire. Now, where was I? Oh, yeah. Me and my friends—you should've seen us, too. We all had on new suits that we had just bought with our oil money. I tell you what, Kone, we were looking like a bunch of long-haired Cary Grants.

"I didn't drum that night, but I do remember the drummers being especially loud, like they were trying to wake the dead or something. Maybe that's what happened. You could just barely hear any singing. Back then, everybody sang, too, and I mean *everybody,* even the little children. I don't know why it's not like that anymore.

"Well, after a while, me and my friends started to socialize, like people do at pow-wows. You know, find out who's marrying who, who just had a baby, and stuff like that. It was already late when the announcer finally declared that it was time for the women's fancy shawl dance, every man's favorite dance. So me and my friends regrouped to watch the women, well, dance. And a whole bunch of them, more than usual, went out to the middle. I guess they all wanted to show off their moves.

"As soon as the drummers got a good song going, the women began dancing. Then one of my friends tapped me on the shoulder and pointed to one particular dancer. She was beautiful, probably the most beautiful Indian woman I had ever seen, next to your grandmother, of course. But this girl was an amazing dancer, too. Me and my friends ended up watching only her because she would glance at us and smile. Boy, you should've seen all of us stand up straight when she did, too. That's what a pretty woman will do to you, Kone. So there we were, our eyes glued to her doing all of these hoss dance moves. But we weren't the only ones checking her out. Almost every man there was in her power.

"The first song went by pretty fast, and then the drummers let the women take a little breather. By this time, me and my friends were asking around, trying to find out who the beautiful one was, but no one knew. That was kind of strange, because everybody knew everybody. The pow-wow circuit wasn't that big yet. Anyways, as soon as the drummers started again, the beautiful one was still the center of attention. Everybody around the circle, mainly all the guys, started singing. And just like that, it became a celebration and we were all celebrating the same thing: the beautiful one's dance moves. There were even guys lined up for a chance to talk to her when she left the circle.

"You should've seen this girl dance. She was better than good. Some shawl dancers got so jealous of her that they left the circle early. But most stayed and tried to outdance her. When that second song got to a full beat, they all started tearing at the earth, putting their tiny moccasins to the test. You know how they do it. The drummers picked up the pace even more, but the dancers were ready. You should've seen them—they were gettin' it. And all we could do was watch with our mouths open, like this, as the beautiful one outdid all of the other women, doing moves no one had even seen before. Unbelievable moves! Swift and cunning moves that brought forth emotions. She was putting tears in our eyes. Smiles on our faces. I'm telling you, Kone. Then the beat got as hard as it could get, hard as it had ever gotten for any fancy shawl dancer. A couple more dancers gave up, but not the beautiful one. It was just her and a few other girls out there. They kept on swinging their shawls and dresses, glorifying the world and everything in it. Finally the beat wasn't even a beat anymore. It was thunder! It was hundreds of atom bombs going off, one after another, until, finally, the only one left out in the circle was the beautiful one. By this time, she was just a blur of colors. And her moves were so powerful, they made everyone watching dance along with her. Really, everybody started to dance, even me! With our bodies in rhythm and our voices in tune, the beautiful one danced like she was bringing the end of the world. Oh, it was a beautiful Armageddon.

"But while I was caught up in my own little

dance, I heard someone yelling. It was my friend and he was pointing. I couldn't hear him, so I got close, close enough to make out his words, which were 'Look at her legs!' I turned in time to see her dress twirl up. That's when I saw her legs, but they weren't human legs. They were all covered with hair and she had hooves. I swear, my heart skipped a beat, and I thought *It can't be*. But it was. Everybody stopped singing. Everybody was seeing what I was seeing! Everybody except the drummers, so they continued drumming and the beautiful one continued dancing. At that point, a young man ran out into the circle and grabbed the hem of the dancer's dress and lifted it for all to see. I have no reason to lie, and swear what I'm going to tell you is the truth, Kone. When that young man pulled her dress up, you could see that she had deer legs. And not just the legs, but the whole lower body of a deer. It was Deer Lady! The most famous shape-shifter of all. She stopped dancing and became angry. So angry that she grabbed that young man's head and pulled it off and threw it into the fire. Everybody started screaming and running every which way, while she went on a murderous rampage, taking the lives of whomever she wished. I barely got away myself. I hid behind a car and watched her trample people and do other bad things to them.

"She is known to collect the juicy parts of people, like the eyes and the tongue, and that's what she was doing, stocking up on both. She was there for a hunt! And no one could leave, because a big pileup wreck had blocked the exit. So she just took her time getting what she wanted. No one was safe from her, not even me.

"But I came to realize that I might be the only one able to do something to chase her away. I was the only medicine man there that night, even though I was still a medicine-man-in-training. And I just happened to have medicine on me, not very powerful medicine, but medicine nonetheless. I knew there was a possibility I could ward her off with the medicine, and as a medicine-man-in-training, it was my duty. I'll tell you what, though: I was scared, and I don't know where I got the courage to stand up and yell at her, but I did, and she heard me. As fast as she could, she galloped toward me. I thought my days were numbered, but I managed to open up my pouch, and as soon as she got close, I threw some medicine at her. It worked, too! It hurt her! She let out this horrible cry and then she started to speak a language I had never heard, so just in case she was trying to put a curse on me, I started a countercurse prayer. I closed my eyes and I prayed and prayed until, finally, I heard the sound of hooves trotting away. I opened my eyes just in time to see her hop back into the woods, wounded.

"We were lucky that night. We had lost some lives, but I had heard many stories where Deer Lady wiped out whole camps. She's an evil being capable of terrible, terrible things. And ever since that night long ago, I have been cursed. You see, I was young and very bad at countercurse prayers. She put a curse on me so that she could find me someday and have her revenge. And that's one thing you don't do is get an evil being like her mad at you. They don't stop hunting you until they get their revenge. So that's why I'm always gone, Kone; I'm still running from her. And she is still tracking me; she never gives up. But I am always one step ahead of her, Kone."

The story sent chills through Mausape's body. It left him speechless. For the rest of the drive, neither one of them said a word. Instead, his grandpa turned the radio on. And he had a weird grin on his face, like he had just done something he had wanted to do for a very, very long time.

That night, when Mausape was in the middle of a dream, he was awakened by the crash of a window being busted out. There were also the sounds of a struggle somewhere. Mausape immediately thought about his grandpa. He shot out of bed and raced to his grandpa's room. There was an unsettling silence coming from the other side of his grandpa's door. Mausape opened it. The room was alive with wind and papers flying everywhere. Glass glittered on the floor. The window was broken. The bed was empty. His grandpa was gone. Mausape knew: Deer Lady had finally caught his grandpa and had taken him on his last trip away from home.

Dancing Days
1990

As color pushed the black sky away, Mausape, now a thirteen-year-old full-blooded X Indian boy, slept quietly in his warm bed. A hand shook him, and he reluctantly opened his eyes. In the pale light, he saw his grandpa standing over him. Sleep overtaking confusion, he closed his eyes again.

"Come on, Kone, wake up," his grandpa ordered him. "You gotta get ready—we have a long journey ahead of us." Mausape pried open his eyes. His grandpa stood beside his bed—dressed, oddly, as if he were on his way to a pow-wow. His long gray hair was parted down the middle and twisted into two long braids, and he was wearing his favorite fancy-dancer outfit. And what a beautiful outfit it was, an attention-demanding display of colored tassels and fine feathers—his favorite among the few he had, mainly because it was red and white, representing the ongoing battle between those two colors of people. Plus, they were the colors of his favorite football team, the Comancheville Chiefs.

"What's going on?" Mausape asked blearily.

"Just hush now and get your fancy-dancer outfit on," his grandpa replied.

Fancy-dancer outfit? Mausape didn't own a fancy-dancer outfit, nor did he fancy-dance. Thinking his grandpa was losing his mind, Mausape slowly got up from his bed and walked over to his wall calendar. January 8, dead in the middle of winter. Pow-wow season was long gone and a long time away. He tried to question his grandpa once more but only got an order to hurry.

Mausape did what he was brought up to do: listen to his elders. He combed his short tangled hair and went to his closet to find something to wear. It was cold, so he needed something warm. He opened his closet, expecting to see his usual mixed pile of clean and dirty clothes. What he saw instead, right in the center of his closet, was the most beautiful fancy-dancer outfit he had ever laid eyes on. The sight of it took his breath away. It couldn't be for him. It was just too much, way too much. He heard his grandpa go outside, so he jumped at the opportunity to try it on, just to see what he would look like in it. After every lace was tied and every button fastened, he looked himself over in an old mirror. Mausape was captured by his own warrior presence. He couldn't look away.

The headdress consisted of a well-designed white-and-turquoise headband, complete with extending white quills. Beautiful shades of green covered the body area, from the feathers protruding in back to the beaded armbands. The leggins were as authentic as they could get. Made out of buffalo fur, they brought the outfit's bright glow to a halt at the knees. And his every movement was signaled by the beautiful sound of four brand-new bell bands around his arms and legs that shone without the slightest smudge. It took him a while to realize it, but he resembled the earth. Maybe Mother Earth herself made the outfit. Hypnotized by the details, Mausape didn't hear his grandpa come back into the room.

"Kone, you look hoss," said his grandpa with an admiring whistle.

"Whose outfit is this, Grandpa?" asked Mausape, bouncing up and down, making the most awe-inspiring noise.

"Yours, of course. A champion outfit for a champion fancy-dancer."

"No, really. Whose is it?" asked Mausape with an unbelieving smile.

"On top of being the best, you're modest. I like that about you, Mausape."

"Modest? You know I can't dance, Grandpa. I mean,

I've always wanted to learn how, but surely I couldn't get an outfit like this just for wanting to learn?"

"Kone, you must've bumped your head in your sleep. Get your stuff ready and just leave that on. We got to get going."

"Where are we going?"

"To Medicine Mountain. It's a long way from NDN City."

"Why are we going there?"

"You really did bump your head, didn't you? Come on, let's go."

Without an explanation, Mausape got ready for the twelve-hour journey. By 5:30 a.m., he was in his grandpa's old tan-and-brown truck and they were off. In silence, they drove away from the Indian neighborhood of Bethlehem, in the Indian town of NDN City, deep inside the Indian Territory—all part of the former Indian land known as America.

They made their way onto the Crazy Horse Turnpike and headed west, like a blood cell through a vein. Along with many other mountains, Medicine Mountain made up the western border of the I.T., or Indian Territory. Car after car sped past Mausape and his grandpa on the turnpike.

"So, what's this all about?" Mausape finally asked.

"You really don't know? It's the King's birthday today and he's challenged you to a contest. Remember?"

"King? What King?"

"The King. You know, the King of All Fancy-Dancers. He's heard so much about your moves. Now he wants to see them for himself."

"You must have bumped *your* head, Grandpa. I don't even dance, so why would I challenge the King of All Fancy-Dancers?"

"What do you mean, you don't dance? What about when you took the prize money at Red Earth and the Gathering of the Nations?"

"Took what?"

"Ah, never mind. You better get some rest—you got a big night ahead of you."

"I am tired, but I'm not dancing in no contest, if that's what you're thinking," mumbled Mausape, leaning against the door of the truck. As he drifted off to sleep, hoping he would awaken in his nice, warm bed, his grandpa hummed old ghost-dance songs about massacring white people.

It seemed to Mausape that he had just closed his eyes when he was being shaken awake by his grandpa yet again. He wiped his eyes to find it was night already. In front of them, lit by the moon, was Medicine Mountain! It was majestic, the biggest thing Mausape had ever seen. They pulled into an open field off an old country road. Mausape heard the sound of a drum pumping like a heartbeat; then, as they drove over a small hill, hundreds and hundreds of cars became visible. They were all parked perfectly around a thicket of trees, where a white glow tried desperately to escape and a trail of both Indians and X-Indians walked to its source.

"Where we at, Grandpa?" asked Mausape, even though he knew.

"The Medicine Mountain dance grounds. Big, ain't it? They're expecting us. Now, if we can just get through this parking lot . . ." And they weaved through the parking lot like a careful needle.

"What time is it?"

"Five thirty."

"Think they got an Indian taco stand somewhere? I'm starving."

"You'll have to eat later. You gotta warm up—we're on in thirty minutes." Then it all came back to Mausape. He looked down and saw that he still had the fancy-dancer outfit on, not to mention the fact that his grandpa did, too! Mausape started to get a little freaked out.

"Grandpa, I don't think this is a good idea. I'll make a fool out of myself."

"Ah, you'll do just fine."

"But I told you, I can't dance. I don't know how."

"Horse rubbish. You can and you will. Because if you don't, we'll be the shame of our people. You don't want that, do you?"

"I can live with that."

"Listen, Kone, you have to beat the King. If not for

yourself, do it for the Territory. Do it for the title that is rightfully ours."

"I'm telling you, Grandpa, I can't do it."

"You must. Hey, here's our parking spot. Listen, we can't turn around now. I know you're scared, but just warm up a little and then see how you feel."

"Okay. But it won't change my mind."

They emerged from the truck, a colorful Indian and his X-Indian grandson. Hope seemed to remain for both dying cultures. They walked to a small building next to the dance grounds. On the way there, Mausape caught a glimpse of the dance circle, which looked to be about a hundred yards in diameter; it was the biggest outdoor dance circle he had ever seen. And sitting on the bleachers placed around the circle, there looked to be at least a thousand people, all watching different kinds of traditional dances. The small building turned out to be a locker room. The warmth inside welcomed them, and was almost enough to distract Mausape's attention from the situation he was in, but then the drums stopped and there was silence. An uneasy feeling ran down Mausape's throat and into his stomach. A voice cut through the silence like a dull knife.

"Ladies and gentlemen! Guys and dolls! The King's showdown is just moments away! I am here to inform you that the fancy-dancer representing the I.T. has just arrived and is now warming up! Also, this just in, tonight is two-for-one snag night! Hear that, guys! When you find you a snag, you get her sister as a bonus! Whee-cha! Drummers! Take it on out!"

"Did you hear that? They think I'm going to dance," said Mausape. His heart started to beat faster than the drums outside.

"Why shouldn't they? You showed up, you have your outfit on, and you're in here, ready to warm up," said his grandpa, who always had a funny way of revealing the truth.

"Yeah, but . . . Grandpa?" Just as he had many times before, Mausape turned to his grandpa for the answer. His grandpa would never lead him astray, never—it was an inborn belief.

"Just warm up and practice your routine. You go on pretty soon."

There was nothing for Mausape to do but find a way to believe in himself, because, well, his grandpa did. Without another question, he started to stretch. After he was done stretching, his grandpa lit some sage in a small tin bowl and feathered smoke around him. Then he carefully placed two medicine pouches in Mausape's leggins, one for each leg. Immediately the medicine began to take over Mausape's legs. Of their own will, they started overlapping each other to the drumbeat outside. Mausape bounced crazily. Then his body went through a series of quick turns. He turned so fast, all he could see were streaks of color. Within minutes he'd gone through a fancy-dance routine for the first time, yet it felt like an old routine he had spent years perfecting. His grandpa watched with a smile. By the time Mausape walked out of that locker room, he was a fancy-dancer.

"Grandpa, your medicine made me feel like I can beat the King of All Fancy-Dancers," declared Mausape.

"That's the spirit, boy! You do this for your people, and they will write great songs about you."

Mausape and his grandpa made their way into the circle like a boxer and his trainer entering the ring. The crowd greeted them with boos and cheers. The MC made his way to the middle of the circle. Mausape was surprised to see that he was none other than the movie actor Gary Farmer; he'd seen him in *Powwow Highway, Smoke Signals,* and some other films.

"Ladies and gentlemen! Guys and dolls! Welcome to the Thunderdome! Where it's going down tonight! The moment you all have been waiting for! The spectacular spectacle! The event to end all events! Two men will enter, but only one man will leave! Gah, not that bad, enit? But tonight, we'll witness the showdown between the King of All Fancy-Dancers and Mausape Onthaw, the little fancy-dancer who could! Or, at least, thought he could! Without further delay, Mr. Onthaw will take the first song, and then birthday boy will be next! Let's dance!"

Mausape gave the drummers the signal to start. They

began to pound softly on their drums, all of them in sync. With confidence, Mausape started off with a slow bounce, the jangle of his bells keeping time with the beat of the drums. Then the beat sped up and grew a little louder. Now Mausape began to overlap his legs, taking one high step over the next. The colorful strings of his outfit came to life. The beat continued to gather speed and strength, and Mausape added more and more fancy moves to his routine. Colors were zooming and zigzagging; bells were ringing and jangling. The crowd grew excited. So did Mausape's legs. When the drummers stuck with a hard rhythm for a short time, Mausape spun round and round and round until he became a tornado of brilliant color. Then the drummers tried to throw him off by coming to an abrupt stop, but Mausape stopped, too, right on a dime, with the beat. The crowd went into a frenzy. After a few beatless verses, the drummers came in again, going at it now with enough determination to wake the dead. The beat got crazy, but Mausape got just as crazy. He started to do flips, one-handed somersaults, and other moves that were very daring, even for fancy-dancers who knew the beat because it could stop at any time, no matter how hard it was pumping. The crowd watched in awe as Mausape gave the best and only performance of his life.

The drummers tried again and again to shake Mausape but failed every time. With only a look they all agreed to try once more, but this time while Mausape tried another flip. He went up for another daring backflip. Just as he threw his body into the air, the beat came to a dead halt. Crickets could be heard. Every spectator was shocked. With his feet pointed toward the sky and his head pointed toward the ground, Mausape had frozen in midair! The silence was thick and suffocating, and the drummers were too flabbergasted to go on. All they could do was witness this miraculous event. Mausape waited a few more seconds for the beat to pick up again, and when it didn't, he flipped back onto his feet. The crowd gave Mausape a standing ovation and then the greatest honor a fancy-dancer could receive after a performance—they threw disks of fry bread at him. He bowed and ran to his grandpa.

"The great and talented Mausape Onthaw, everybody!" Gary Farmer yelled into a microphone. "Dang, that was one impressive routine! That's what it's all about! Give him a hand!" The crowd's clapping grew even louder. "But now—you know him, you love him, you can't fuckin' live without him! Make way for the King!"

While Mausape was wiping the sweat off his face with a towel, he watched the crowd part. The King of All Fancy-Dancers was coming, and Mausape was about to get his first glimpse of him. The drums started again, but this time to a slow beat. Mausape thought the beat was familiar.

Bumm . . . bummmmmmmm! Bumm . . . bummmmmmmm!

Bumm . . . bummmmmmm! went the drums. Everyone went nuts.

Like Moses parting the Red Sea and walking on through, here came the King. Mausape's first glimpse of the large Caucasian man who held the title the King of All Fancy-Dancers helped him recognize that beat. It was "Jailhouse Rock"! All of the sudden, a spotlight found the man, the myth. The King of All Fancy-Dancers was none other than Elvis Presley! And it wasn't Elvis in his early years, but the Vegas Elvis, bright as the lights of Las Vegas itself. The crowd went totally insane as he started the first verse of "Jailhouse Rock."

Mausape watched, just as excited as the crowd. The King swung one leg in circles and swung an arm along with it. It was simple but mesmerizing. And Mausape couldn't keep his eyes off the King's outfit. It was made of fancy white leather, with everything from jewels to decorative writing all over it. On the back, written in rhinestones, was "The King." To complete the luxurious outfit, the zipper of his jacket was made of gold. It was, by far, the best fancy-dancer outfit Mausape had ever seen. And the high he'd been on since he started dancing quickly faded.

The King of All Fancy-Dancers was the King for a reason. Mausape used medicine to help his moves, but the King's moves were medicine itself—so powerful it could heal the sick, make the cripple stand, and bring joy to the most depressed. Mausape watched the King end his routine, more as a spectator than as an adversary. And what an ending it was—even more spectacular than Mausape's. As the last beat hit, sparks flew up in the air behind him and a sign was set ablaze. It read THE KING IS HERE. But the King didn't end his show there. No, he went right into another song-and-dance routine. The soft beat and sound of "Love Me Tender" filled the night and set a romantic mood. People sat closer together. And as the King made his way around the circle, the ladies went ballistic. Even old war mothers tugged at Elvis, and, just as he was known for doing, he touched their faces, sending them one by one into small convulsions and unconsciousness.

After every lady had passed out at least once and every man had envied him just a little, Elvis finished. Like a true sportsman, Elvis Presley, the King, strode gracefully toward Mausape. Mausape grew weak in the knees.

"Thank you, thank you very much. Good luck," said the King as he winked at Mausape and shook his hand.

"Yeah, good luck, sir," was all Mausape could get out.

By the time the King made it back to his side, the MC was already in the middle of the circle again. Mausape didn't see the point of wasting everyone's time, because it was obvious who the winner was. He crossed his fingers, hoping that maybe they would just give the trophy or belt to Elvis and save him the shame, but it was an unanswered hope.

"We had a doozy here, didn't we? So, before I announce the winner, give the King and his challenger a hand for their efforts!" Gary Farmer set off a roar from the crowd. Then he pulled out an envelope from inside his jean jacket, opened it, and began to read: "By an anonymous decision from our judges, the winner is . . ."

"Mausape! Mausape!" yelled a familiar voice.

Mausape reluctantly opened his eyes, confusion overtaking sleep. His grandma was standing over him.

"What?" he softly asked.

"Get up, it's time for school!" shouted his grandma, who always started her day by shouting at him to get up. It was an old method, passed down from ancestors of long ago, but it still worked. His grandma was a short Indian woman with sharp, pointy glasses and salt-and-pepper hair.

"School?"

"Yeah, school! You're not missing today. It's picture day, so get up and dress nice!"

Mausape didn't put up a struggle, as he usually did, and his grandma left the room. He dragged himself to his closet, but once there, he remembered the dream he had. Was it a dream? He opened his closet, hoping to see the fancy-dancer outfit, but found nothing except for the mixed pile of clean and dirty clothes. It broke his heart; he had missed his grandpa so since his death or disappearance exactly five years earlier. Mausape knew his grandma didn't care that it was picture day. January 8 was a day of mourning for her, and she liked to be alone.

Mausape found his best clothes and got dressed. The sound of his grandma cooking got his stomach's attention, so he quickly made his way into the kitchen of their small Indian home. A plate of powdered eggs, mixed with real scrambled eggs, and a bowl of farina were waiting for him on their simple dining table. Mausape began to scarf down his breakfast as if he really had been fancy-dancing all night.

"Grandma, did Grandpa ever fancy-dance?" he asked through a mouthful of farina.

"Why, yes, he did. You know, at one time, he was one of the best fancy-dancers in the whole Territory, except it was called war-dancing then. Why, what makes you ask?" She took a seat across from him.

"No reason, really. Actually, I was wondering, how do you become a fancy-dancer?"

"Oh, you have to be taught by an elder. It's a long process. You know, your grandpa taught a lot of dancers."

"Did he ever teach you anything about it?"

"Of course not. Fancy-dancing is a man's dance. But I was a pretty good fancy shawl dancer. As a matter of fact, that's how we met, at this pow-wow where we both took first."

"Gah, you and Grandpa were pow-wow snags?"

"No. Well, sort of."

"I gotta hear this. What happened?"

"Oh, it's a good one. We both took first place at this pow-wow, so they made us lead a round dance together, and the whole time, your grandpa just stared at me. He was such a handsome man. Well, afterwards, he tried to talk to me, but I wasn't all that interested. But after that, he somehow ended up at every pow-wow I danced at. And in every contest he danced in, he would always win first place in my honor, or so he said. It took a long time, but one night, he finally gathered enough courage to ask me out on a date. It's all he had to do in the first place, instead of trying to show off in front of me, like I was going to run into his arms or something. When he finally asked me, we were at a small pow-wow, one we were both sure to win. So I made a deal with him: if he took first place in my honor one last time, I would go on a date with him."

"I bet Grandpa was on fire that night," said Mausape.

"You'd think, but it was actually quite the opposite. I guess it made him nervous or something. Before, he won just to impress me. But now I'd put more on the line for him. Oh, his routine was terrible. He fumbled moves, he was off beat, and God knows what else. He did so bad, he was too ashamed to even talk to me afterwards. I felt so sorry for him, too, because I knew it was my fault that he'd lost. So that night, I went and found him and I apologized. He was so heartbroken, I couldn't help but tell him that I would still go on a date with him. But he didn't have any money to take me out. He had planned on using the prize money he should've won to take me out. So the next night, we just ended up going back to the same pow-wow together. Not as dancers but as visitors. We never got to just sit there and watch like that."

"But both of you did dance again, right?"

"Oh, yeah. We practically raised your father on prize money. You know, now that I think of it, your grandpa did teach you a little."

"He did?"

"Yeah, but then your dad and momma moved, and we never saw too much of you after that until, you know, the accident. But by that time, your grandpa was on the run from you-know-who."

"I wish he could've taught me more."

"He wanted to, but he didn't get to do a lot of things he wanted to do."

"Do you think I can still learn how?"

"Sure, but it's not an easy road to travel. You see, every time an elder like your grandpa passes on to the next world, they take more of our culture with them. A lot has already gone to the next world for good, and only so much is left here for people your age to learn. It's so sad. Your generation is going through the future with very little of your past. But if you really, really want to learn—"

Before Mausape's grandma could finish, there was a

familiar knock at the door. Mausape shot up from his chair and rushed to answer it.

"Well, I gotta go, Grandma!" he shouted as he opened the door.

"Don't forget to smile!" she yelled back.

Mausape was greeted on the porch by his best friend, Marlon Buffalo. They were both thirteen, but Marlon was a monster compared with Mausape—tall, plump, built for war. He was a true X-Indian, long hair pulled back into a braided ponytail and everything. And by the look of the clothes he had on—a blue polo shirt, tan khakis, loafers— his mother also knew it was picture day. Even with his old jean jacket on over his picture-day attire, he could have passed for civilized, but he was far from it.

The two teenagers took their usual early-morning trip to the bus stop.

"I had a jacked-up dream last night," Mausape blurted out. It was almost too cold to talk.

"What was it about?" Marlon asked with his usual raspy voice.

"My grandpa."

"For reals? My mom told me that when you see dead people in your dreams, they're usually trying to tell you something, warn you."

"It felt so real, though. Damn, I don't even feel like going to school today."

"Fuck it, let's ditch."

"I would, but my grandma'll find out if she don't get my pictures."

"Oh, yeah, my mom, too." They walked a few feet in silence. "Hey, man, I just happen to have something that'll cheer you up."

"What's that?" Mausape asked.

Marlon pulled something out of his pocket. "Check it out," he said, and held up something totally unexpected. In front of Mausape's virgin eyes was a nicely rolled marijuana joint. It was intriguing. It was intimidating. Most of all, it was new. They had never smoked weed, but, like cats are, they were curious.

"Where'd you get that?" Mausape asked.

"Stole it from my dad. I raided his stash this morning while he was passed out."

"You're fuckin' crazy."

"Ah, he won't miss it. He's got pounds of this stuff at home. So, you wanna get high or what?"

"Now?"

"After school, fool. Rodney and James might want to get in on this, too."

Rodney and James were the other half of what junior-high counselors referred to as their peer group. They lived across town in another neighborhood called Jerusalem.

"I'm down with it."

"Fuckin' A, you better be. We are going to get so high!" Marlon shouted. Cheered up, Mausape smiled. It was a very entertaining thought, their getting high for the first time.

When they got to the bus stop, they joined the other X-Indian kids there, all dressed in their best rags, all waiting for a free ride to assimilation.

ANOTHER FANCY-DANCER LOST

Cowman
1991

In the beginning, after the Great Spirit had made everything that is, was, and will be, he took a day of rest. Predators and prey had all been assigned, and the first ancestor of every plant and animal knew how the food chain worked. But it was the spirit of the first cow that went up to the Great Spirit on this day and questioned him. The spirit of the cow asked its maker if it could have its own special kind of meat to eat, because the task of eating grass was a very slow one.

The Great Spirit looked at the spirit of the cow and asked what it had in mind. The spirit of the cow carefully explained how it needed something really nutritious for its large body. Something with plenty of muscle meat, with a good mixture of fatty meat, and neither too big nor too small, maybe something like . . . a human being. The spirit of the cow decided that humans would be the perfect delicacy.

On this same day, Tahlee, the spirit of the first man, went up to the Great Spirit and asked if he could have a more fulfilling meat. Tahlee felt that, even though chicken, fish, and other animals' meat was good, it didn't quite satisfy his hunger. As men do, he wanted more.

The Great Spirit then looked at Tahlee and asked what he had in mind. Tahlee went on to describe his craving for a really red and fatty meat. He went on to tell the Great Spirit how he wanted an animal that offered a surplus of meat so that he didn't have to hunt so much. It had to be as slow as it was big—an easy catch. Then Tahlee looked at the spirit of the cow and decided it fit his description.

The Great Spirit thought about the two wishes and concluded that the cow and Tahlee each had a strong case. But the Great Spirit knew he couldn't give both of them what they wanted, because it would upset the balance and they'd wipe each other out. The Great Spirit loved his creations equally, so it was a hard decision. It was a decision that could only be solved one way, through a competition. The competition could not be one of strength, because Tahlee was no match for the spirit of the cow. Nor could the competition be one of wits, because the spirit of the cow was no match for Tahlee. The Great Spirit struggled over a choice of competition until he decided to just create one. Thus was conceived a guessing game called the handgame by Indians and X-Indians alike.

To determine who would be the guesser, the Great Spirit had the two choose a number between one and one hundred. The spirit of the cow chose fifty, while Tahlee chose seven. The winning number was one, so Tahlee would be the one to choose their fate. The spirit of the cow was given a small stick to hold in one of its hands and to try to trick Tahlee into guessing incorrectly. The Great Spirit announced that if Tahlee did, in fact, choose the hand holding the stick, he would get his wish. If Tahlee chose the empty hand, the spirit of the cow would get its wish.

Their hearts began to beat hard together; the sound of drums was thunderous. The spirit of the cow cleverly switched the stick from hand to hand, to his left, to his right, behind his back. Instead of watching the stick, Tahlee watched the eyes of the spirit of the cow. That was where he was going to find the stick.

Finally, the spirit of the cow stopped. As it held out its hands for Tahlee to guess, the drumming got louder. All the while, Tahlee stared into the spirit of the cow's cold, dark eyes. He reached for the left hand but hesitated after he saw a hint of a grin on the spirit of the cow's face.

Then he reached for the right hand and saw what he needed to see, panic. Tahlee touched the right hand of the spirit of the cow.

The Great Spirit ordered the spirit of the cow to open its right hand, and as it did, the stick became visible. There was a smile and there was a frown as the Great Spirit announced that the cow would become the primary source of meat for human beings and would remain a harmless plant eater. The spirit of the cow, feeling outsmarted, swore revenge, and a curse was put in place where it was least expected—on cows.

Marlon, Mausape, Rodney, and James had heard the Cowman story time and time again. From what they knew, Cowman was supposed to be the spirit of the cow in mortal form. His appearance was said to be appalling; it was said that he was almost a man, except his legs were covered in hair, his feet were hooves, and his head was that of a cow, similar to the Minotaur in Greek mythology. The story was that Cowman could only be resurrected when someone disrespected a cow. To disrespect a cow was to say a "thanks for nothing" prayer over a meal, something the Great Spirit didn't appreciate all that much. It was said that if someone did disrespect a cow, Cowman would do the unthinkable—he would let his cows taste that person's flesh, seeing how human flesh was the only meat cows ever considered eating. Stories of Cowman encounters were rare in the Indian Territory and almost nonexistent in NDN City. But there was this one story, one in which some boys learned a lesson in death.

It happened one hot July night in 1991. There were five X-Indian boys to begin with, all of them not older than fifteen: Marlon, Mausape, Rodney, James, and Kevin, who were doing nothing more than waiting on an opportunity to cause mischief. It's what they did.

They were all staying the night at Kevin's house; he was half-white and lived far out in the country, dead in the middle of nowhere. From his house, NDN City was just an orange glow on the horizon. But they liked it out there. Where else could they spend the whole day riding dirt bikes and ATVs, like adolescent versions of Hell's Angels?

Marlon, Mausape, Rodney, and James had never known anybody like Kevin. He was rich with possessions and poor in the things that most teenagers hated, like rules, chores, and discipline. Both his parents worked and never seemed to be home. The four boys thought Kevin was as lucky as anybody could get.

Saddle sore from the vibrating motors of their small horses, they stopped to rest in a field near Kevin's house. Thoughts of what to do next were out there in the stars above them, waiting. It was Kevin who grabbed the first idea and the boys were game; it was better than nothing.

Quickly, they conjured up a lifelike dummy of a person, which they were going to place in the middle of the road, halfway down Tickle Hill, so that when cars drove down the hill, they would hit it and think it was a person. And just like they planned it, it worked. People freaked out! Some stopped and panicked; others just got the hell out of there. The boys pulled it off more times than they should've and got the laughs they were craving, but, like all things, it got boring fast and they quit.

Once more, the five troublemakers were without anything to do. It was Kevin again who came up with another sick and twisted idea. He reminded the boys of a herd of cattle they had passed in a field close to his house, and went on to suggest that they sneak up on the cows, push one over, and saw its leg off with a chain saw he had. Then they would ride down to Jeremiah's Bridge and hang the leg from one of the rails above the bridge. The next day, when someone found it, people would think Jeremiah, the ghost that haunted that particular bridge, had ripped the leg off the cow. It was said that Jeremiah would appear to anyone who called his name three times, then tear their limbs off. And that was why the prank was so genius. There was no way a cow could say "Jeremiah" three times.

The boys were impressed by Kevin's cleverness and helped him carry his chain saw through moonlit fields to the cows. When they got to the cows, though, they could all feel it, even smell it—death was in the air. It was enough to make Marlon, Mausape, Rodney, and James chicken out, but Kevin insisted that there was nothing to worry about. Only a cow was doomed that night.

The white person in Kevin pushed him to approach the cows alone. His friends watched from about a hundred yards away, in a thicket of trees. But because the moon was shining bright, they could see clearly. Kevin was always trying to prove himself, always trying to show them that he was just as brave as a full-blood. The boys always got a good kick out of him.

Kevin was out for blood. The boys watched as an unlucky cow hit the ground. The sound of a chain saw sent the cows running for their lives, but one pleading moo rang out. Then blood flew at the moon and at the stars, and all of the sudden, there was a loud crunch.

The other cows stopped running then and did something strange—they turned as one to face Kevin. The boys didn't like what they were seeing; the cows were standing up against their friend. The cows weren't afraid anymore. No. Now they were out for blood. But only one cow went forward, and it caught all four boys' attention. From the middle of the herd, one cow rose above the rest and made its way swiftly toward Kevin as if it were running on two legs. But that was impossible!

The boys quickly grew afraid. They could barely manage to whisper at Kevin to run. But Kevin was deafened by his own glory. He was king of his domain; he was a true warrior, holding a cow leg raised high above his head to prove it. By this time, the tall cow had emerged from the herd and was sprinting toward Kevin. Right before the boys' unbelieving eyes, the dark humanlike figure with cow legs and a cow head ran up to their friend.

Kevin never saw it coming. Cowman pushed him from behind and threw him to the ground with tremendous force. He stomped in Kevin's head with his hooves. The gruesome scene sent the four boys into shock. They saw it all—the blood flying at the moon and the twitching limbs, then the lifeless body of their friend being dragged to the cows. And that was where he did it. That was where Cowman skinned Kevin. An evil moo echoed across the plains, and the whole herd feasted. Overeager, they snarled and they chewed, and they consumed Kevin's skinless body.

There was a lot of commotion, grisly commotion— enough to give the boys a chance to pull themselves together and sneak back to Kevin's house, where they drove two of his dirt bikes into town to tell their story to the police, who thought they were either doing drugs or creating their own alibi. It was the kind of story guilty troublemakers would make up to cover a homicide. So the police investigated it and even came upon the mutilated cow, the chain saw, and Kevin's bones. Blood-soaked hoof prints were all over the crime scene. Otherwise, there was no clear evidence of what really happened. Or at least what the police *assumed* had happened.

Regardless, they arrested Marlon, Mausape, Rodney, and James for murder, accusing them of being in some kind of satanic cult and sacrificing Kevin's body to the devil. After a long trial, the boys were found innocent, but the judge recommended that they leave the public school system and be sent to the Rugged Indian Boarding School. It was a haven for X-Indians like themselves, so they would fit in perfectly. And so assimilation was exchanged for decimation.

Kevin's murder was never solved. It was never even spoken of again. Most murders in NDN City never are.

PART II
NDN City

Nitty-gritty

NDN City

Winos

Bibles

Atheists

Tribal

Fry bread born

Indian corn

Sirens

Screams

Diabetes

Methamphetamine

Pow-wow songs

Indian homes

War parties

Vision quests

Welfare

DNA tests

Another elder dies

Indian 49

Buffalo

Bingo

Sweat lodge

Casino

Flowing rivers

Indian giver

A head-on crash

A DUI

A gunshot blast

A mother's cry

Violent bars

Indian cars

The future

The past

No credit

No cash

An unpaid fine

Indian time

My Favorite Runner
1995

Indians of the past were known to be great distance runners, but there is another breed of runners most X-Indians have grown to know. These runners are the ones who purchase alcohol for minors. As a compulsive-drinking minor in NDN City, James, whose street name was Maddog, knew many runners. During his eighteenth year, when he was making mad money from selling drugs, he did as most drug dealers did: he partied his ass off. But because he wasn't yet old enough to buy alcohol, runners were a must. Although most were a dime a dozen to him, Maddog did have one favorite—a runner who once won a race for their race.

Maddog's favorite runner's name was Tricky Heights, a.k.a. the town crazy. Most thought him to be way over forty, but the truth was, he was only thirty-six years old. And even though he was in his midthirties, his mind was still grade-school young. His state of mind had always been a subject of debate in NDN City. Some said he had always been like that, and some said that he'd gone on an acid trip and never come back. The way he dressed could have been proof of the acid trip theory. He always wore ugly-colored slacks, outlandish cowboy shirts, and a pair of shiny cowboy boots. A lot of people said Tricky looked like a strung-out cowboy version of Squiggy from the TV show *Laverne & Shirley.* And Tricky was never without his trademark cigarette or his small radio or his habit of walking fast. He was a complicated yet simple man.

It was never hard to find him, either, because he only hung out at one particular convenience store, the Stop-N-Grab-M, where he bummed change. That was where Maddog first asked Tricky to buy him some beer.

"If it ain't ole Tricky Heights!" Maddog yelled in a joking manner from inside his best friend Rodney's car, Silver, a gray '84 Cutlass Supreme. Maddog was a scary-looking X-Indian—tall, dark, and thick, a hard thick— who didn't much care how he dressed. Most people knew Maddog as being a brute, but Tricky thought of him as generous, and went to greet him.

"Hey, *piah-phee,* w-what are you d-doing?" Tricky Heights asked. He always spoke fast.

"We're tryin' to get our drink on," Maddog answered

with a smile. He was always in good spirits. "What about you?" Rodney, whose street name was Hoss, sat behind the wheel. If being bald was beautiful, Maddog and Hoss were double the fun.

"You g-got any change, *piah-phee*? I need to g-get some g-gas for my car. It b-broke down in the country."

"Don't pull that shit on me, Tricky, I know you ain't got a car. I'll tell you what, though, if you can just tell me the truth, I'll hook you up, *piah-phee*," Maddog offered. He actually liked Tricky, enough to even buy him a beer.

"Okay, *piah-phee*, I want to g-get a beer for the road, I g-got a long walk home t-to the country," said Tricky, reeking of mouthwash and cigarettes.

"Hoss, I don't think Tricky could tell the truth if his life depended on it. Ain't that right, Trick-dog? Man, I know you don't live in no damn country."

"Sorry, *piah-phee*. You g-got some change?"

"Yo, dog. He might be able to help us out with our little situation," Hoss said to Maddog. Hoss was wearing his usual wife-beater T-shirt. He liked to show off his muscles, and X-Indian women loved to admire them. But most X-Indian women would agree that his best feature was his smile. Oh, his smile. They were all in love with it, which revealed a pair of cute dimples. Sometimes, that smile and those dimples were all it took to get a girl to spread her legs for him. But the thing was, he rarely smiled, and almost never in public.

"No shit, huh? Hey, Tricky."

"W–what, *piah-phee*?"

"If you do us a favor, we'll buy you a whole forty."

"What k–kind of f–favor?"

"Just go in there and buy us some beer, that's all," Maddog said, assuming Tricky would easily take the bait. But Tricky had to think about it. He might be slow, but he knew right from wrong and he pondered the consequences. It gave him an idea.

"Okay, *piah-phee,* b–but I was w–wondering if you can d–do something else for me?"

"What's that?" Maddog asked, not really paying any attention. He was too busy reaching into his baggy-ass jeans to get some money.

"C–can you c–comb my hair like Elvis?"

"Yeah, sure. Wait, what was that?"

"C–comb my hair like Elvis."

"Comb your hair like Elvis! Man, what kind of shit is that, Tricky?" Then he and Hoss burst out laughing. Tricky waited patiently and didn't answer until the laughing stopped.

"C–can you, *piah-phee*?"

"You're serious, ain't you? Fuck it. All right, Tricky. You go get our beer and we'll comb your hair like Elvis." Maddog agreed only because they really needed the beer; they had some fine *my-ees* waiting on them back at Maddog's pad. And so Tricky walked inside the Stop-N-

Grab-M and bought Maddog and Hoss a thirty-pack of Brewer's beer and a forty-ounce for himself. Maddog and Hoss hid the beer inside Silver's trunk.

"C-can you c-comb my hair now, *piah-phee?*" asked Tricky, with a childlike sparkle in his eyes that Maddog couldn't resist.

"My word's my bond, man. Let's go in the alley," he said. Hoss and Tricky followed Maddog to the alley, both on the lookout for police. It was a reflex. Tricky's radio was blaring out some bullshit country music.

Tricky found a milk crate and took a seat on it, while Maddog looked around for something to comb Tricky's tangled hair with. After a short search, he found two Popsicle sticks and decided they would do. With a stick in each hand, he started sculpting Tricky's hair. But what did he know about fixing hair? He'd been bald for as long as he could remember. He finished as fast as he could, not wasting too much time on what could never be. Tricky's greasy hair was that hopeless.

"Muthafucker looks like an Indian Elvis Presley, don't he?" Maddog asked Hoss. Hoss pursed his lips and nodded in agreement. His dimples were showing.

"Ah-ho, *p-piah-phee,* th-thank you," Tricky said. He grabbed his radio and quickly paced off with the funkiest hairdo either of them had ever seen.

"Tricky walking like he's about to go get him some," said Hoss.

"Shit, he couldn't show his hand a good time. And speakin' of a good time, we'd better get back to our *my-ees*," Maddog reminded his friend.

As Maddog's sin-filled adolescent days passed, the parties kept going and going and the demand for beer kept coming and coming. Every time he needed a runner for any alcoholic beverage, he would go and find Tricky, who was always down to help an X-Indian out. And after a while, he even stopped charging Maddog beer. As long as he got his hair combed like Elvis, he was a happy camper.

Their little deal was on the down low, but sometimes Maddog had *my-ees* with him when he connected with Tricky. It never failed—the *my-ees* ended up asking Maddog why he and Tricky went behind the store after a buy and why Tricky's hair was always fucked up when they came back. But it was their little secret, their little pact. So Maddog never told any of them, no matter how much they begged.

Maddog kept in good relations with Tricky, and the word hit the streets, like it always did in NDN City, that Tricky was *his* runner. They were friends, too, and anybody that was a friend of Maddog's had few enemies to worry about. With that kind of backup, Tricky wasn't afraid to go into neighborhoods he was once scared to bum in.

Maddog was glad to offer his protection, but never in his wildest dreams did he think he'd ever have to back

Tricky up for real. That was until one day when Tricky told Maddog and Hoss about some white boys who were making a habit of chasing him down like an animal and shooting him with BB guns. They always got him in the afternoon, near his neighborhood, Jerusalem. Maddog hated white boys and that news just fed the fire.

One humid day later, Hoss and Maddog were cruisin' around, smoking weed and looking for the fools that were fucking with Tricky. From a distance, they spotted Tricky walking along the small road that zigzagged toward Jerusalem like an old snake. Maddog and Hoss pulled into an abandoned gas station that overlooked the small stretch of road. They lit another joint to kill a few minutes and watched Tricky walk home. Maddog had a feeling they were at the right place at the right time.

Hoss was just about ready to give up and pull out when a dark blue '66 Mustang came blazing out of Jerusalem like sudden death, toward Tricky. A BB gun barrel emerged from the driver's window. Before Maddog could blink an eye, Tricky became a whole different kind of runner—a running-for-his-life runner. It was as if Jim Thorpe had possessed his legs. From where they were parked, Maddog and Hoss cheered Tricky on and laughed their asses off. It was some funny shit.

Maddog knew the Mustang and the driver, a clean-cut white boy named Biff, with dirty-blond hair and preppy clothes. He was never without his sidekick, Lyle, who looked just like Biff, except for being a brunet. Biff and Maddog had once played football together, when Maddog used to go to public school in NDN City. Biff was a spoiled piece of shit, a straight momma's boy, the kind who would die without his momma. Maddog disliked Biff and Biff knew it. Which was probably why Biff kissed Maddog's ass every time they crossed paths. Like most white boys did when they talked to guys of darker color. Maddog and Hoss reviewed the situation and decided to turn the tables around for greater amusement. Hoss started Silver and off they went, following their friend.

Tricky ran through the run-down neighborhood of Eden, sometimes called Cracktown, where most of the black people in NDN City lived. He ran through messy yards, between crack houses, around closed buildings, and across narrow streets. He made it to the next neighborhood, Nazareth, and it was in the fairgrounds on the outskirts of Nazareth that the pursuit finally ended. There wasn't a fair around or any event taking place—just wide open space in all directions, which left Tricky with nowhere to hide and no way to outsmart his pursuers. He stopped running and the Mustang pulled up beside him. The two white boys got out and eagerly approached their prey. Each draped an arm around Tricky's neck as if they were *piah-phees* of his.

Maddog and Hoss were still keeping their distance, waiting for the right moment. Maddog rarely got angry, but this was too much. He got to thinking about how many times white muthafuckers got away with messing with Indians or X-Indians. He knew that if either kind of Indian fucked with a white person, the police would show up in a heartbeat, ready to haul their Indian asses to jail.

After a brief conversation with Tricky, the two white boys blindfolded him and let him march away. The air filled with their laughter, and they both cocked their BB guns. At that moment Hoss put the pedal to the metal and sped toward them like Mario Andretti on meth. He was as pissed as Maddog, maybe more. Silver surprised the hell out of Biff and Lyle. They were even more surprised to see Maddog and Hoss get out of the car.

"Hey, what's going on, Maddog?" asked Biff, whose pale skin suddenly turned pink. He was definitely afraid.

"What the fuck y'all doin'?" Maddog asked, staring into their disrespectful eyes. He loved seeing the fear there.

"We're just having a little fun," said Biff in a girlish tone. "Check this out." He pointed his gun at Tricky.

"What the fuck you doin'?" Maddog shouted. "That's my uncle, muthafucker!" Before Biff could react, Maddog jerked the BB gun out of his hands. Hoss grabbed Lyle's. It was on.

"Oh, dude, I didn't know he was your uncle," Biff quickly replied. "I was just playing."

"Yeah, Maddog. We weren't trying to hurt him,"

Lyle added. "They're just BB guns." It was pretty obvious that Lyle had already shit his pants.

"No shit, Sherlock. Uncle Tricky! Take that damn thing off and get over here!" Maddog yelled. Tricky took the blindfold off and was overjoyed to see that Maddog had come to the rescue.

"H-hey, *piah-phee*," Tricky greeted him, with a smile from sideburn to sideburn.

"These the fools you said were fucking with you?" Maddog asked.

"Yeah, th-that's the car."

"Man, why are y'all fucking with Tricky? 'Cause he's Native? 'Cause he's poor? Y'all don't like poor Natives, or what?"

"Let's fuck 'em up, dog," suggested Hoss, who always got a little crazy off weed. Actually, he was just a mean little muthafucker. Even though he was the ladies' man of the bunch, he loved to kick ass.

"Wait! Now, there's no need to trip. We're sorry," Biff apologized. He was far from the protection of his mother now.

"Fuck it," said Maddog. "Hoss, by the time we get done with them today, they ain't going to like any kind of Native, especially us."

"Maddog, we don't want any trouble," Biff said. "You can have the guns. We'll just go ahead and leave."

And the two white boys turned to walk back to their car like it was all over. It was a sad attempt.

"Nah, fuck that! Y'all muthafuckers better get y'alls asses back over here," Maddog ordered, "or I'm going to fuck y'all up real bad." Immediately they stopped in their tracks and returned. Maddog was not a person to be taken lightly. He always meant what he said.

"Come on, Maddog," pleaded Lyle, "we said we're sorry."

"To me, but I ain't the one y'all should be apologizin' to."

"We're sorry, Tricky. We were just fucking around," apologized Biff, but in a way that said he wasn't really sorry, just scared. That pissed Maddog off more.

"I think y'all should compensate him."

"Hell yeah," agreed Hoss.

"I got thirty dollars, how's that?" asked Biff.

"Yeah, *p-piah-phee,* yeah, *p-piah-phee,*" said Tricky. It was music to his ears.

"No, something more than money."

"Th-they can c-comb my hair l-like Elvis," suggested Tricky.

"Hey, that's a good idea, Uncle. All right, you two, you heard him! He wants his hair combed like Elvis."

"What?" Lyle asked, not sure if Maddog was for reals.

"You heard him. Now comb his hair like Elvis!"

Biff and Lyle didn't bother trying to argue their way out of it. Reluctantly they pulled out their fancy combs. After Tricky took a seat on the hood of their car, they studied his greasy hair carefully. Then they started sculpting it. They tried a few different parts until finally deciding on one. After that, they twirled, they turned, they combed. In a few minutes they were done. It was good, but not good enough for Maddog, so he made them do it again, and then again. It was on their fourth attempt that magic happened. They had miraculously fixed Tricky's hair so that it resembled the way Vegas Elvis used to wear his hair. It was unbelievable! Tricky really looked like the King!

"Damn," was all Maddog could say.

"I wouldn't have believed it if I didn't see it with my own eyes," said Hoss.

"So, what do you think, Hoss? Should we let them go?"

"I don't know. We still need to teach their asses a lesson."

"What do you mean?"

"Watch this. Hey, y'all two turn around," Hoss ordered.

"Wait, w-we did what you said," Lyle snapped at them, as if he had rights.

"Muthafucker, did he stutter?" Maddog asked, furious.

Biff and Lyle slowly turned around as Hoss handed his

fully loaded BB gun to Tricky, who looked like he had waited his whole life for that moment.

"It's on you, Tricky," Hoss said. "This is your chance to get these white pieces of shit back. Go ahead and bust some BBs into their ass."

"O-k-kay, *piah-phee.*" Tricky pumped the BB gun a few times, then fired and shot Biff right in the ass. Biff jerked and his butt cheeks tightened up. After that, Tricky went off like some trigger-happy psycho, pumping and shooting over and over. Maddog and Hoss had the time of their lives watching him empty the BBs into their asses. Throughout the whole ordeal, Biff and Lyle took the pain and humiliation with a sportsmanship their daddies would have been proud of. By the time Maddog and Hoss allowed them to turn back around, they were the ugliest pink. Shame and hate didn't mix well.

"What's a matter, man? We were just playin'," Maddog said with a smile. "We weren't trying to hurt you—they're just BB guns." Then he started to pump his BB gun, and in a quick draw, he shot Biff right in the balls.

"Okay, we get your point, Maddog," Lyle said, cupping his family jewels.

"Good. If I hear about y'all doing this shit again, y'all are going to wish I was carrying just a BB gun. Now take y'alls' asses back to Babylon!" Maddog yelled. The two white boys scurried back to Biff's Mustang and got the hell out of there. It was the fastest Maddog, Hoss, and Tricky had ever seen white boys move.

As soon as they were gone, Maddog and Tricky put the BB guns into Silver's trunk and drove off to the nearest liquor store, to celebrate their small but meaningful victory. Maddog and Hoss had helped their runner win a race for their race.

Where Are Our Warriors?
1995

Hoss, Maddog, and Tricky decided they wanted gin to celebrate that victory of theirs, the one that involved a pair of BB guns and a pair of spoiled white boys. The nearest liquor store happened to be the nameless liquor store, a.k.a. the Candy Store.

While Maddog made sure Tricky had the order right, Hoss reflected on the situation they had just driven off from. He wasn't sure if it was because of the weed he had smoked earlier or what, but he was paranoid. Sooner or later, the white boys might retaliate, and if so, Hoss knew he had to be ready. That got him thinking about the old days, when men were warriors and had ways to prepare for upcoming battles. Hoss had none. Questions raced through his mind, questions about his warriorism.

Maddog could see something was up with his best friend, because as soon as Tricky was inside the store, Hoss said, "I need to go see Grandma Spider for a minute. Be right back, dog," and got out of the car.

Most thought Hoss to be a little on the soft side, but that wasn't the case. He was as tough as he was short, as tough as he was handsome; a fierce fighter with an ill temper. But there was something deep inside his gut that was not supposed to be there. Warriors weren't supposed to feel fear. It could get them killed, which led to the question lingering in Hoss's mind. Was he a warrior? Grandma Spider would know.

"Man, what for?" asked Maddog, a little over-concerned.

"I'm just going to ask her some shit about being a warrior."

"A warrior? What the fuck? We need to get the hell out of here, for reals. Them white muthafuckers might've called the pigs."

"Fuck the pigs. It'll just take a little bit."

"Then hurry your ass up. Shit, I'm ready to get my drink on."

Some believed Grandma Spider to be nothing but a myth, a piece of a story that had ceased to be told. But she was real; all Indians and some X-Indians knew this to be true. She was one of the wisest beings still alive, although age and civilization had deteriorated her lifestyle. Instead of taking the shape of a spider, she walked the Indian Territory as an old woman. And she began to walk on six spiderlike legs when her body became obese from the endless consumption of alcohol. And instead of taking refuge somewhere on Medicine Mountain or in the Massacre Hills, she hid in the darkest of shadows. Most of the time, behind the nameless liquor store.

That was where Hoss found Grandma Spider doing what she did best them days, drinking. She and two on-call warriors named Swino and Thotes were passing around a green bottle of Thunderbird. The three of them stood in a circle, singing old Ghost Dance songs and stomping their feet on broken glass. The song they sang, translated into English, was "Die, White Muthafuckers! Die!" Only after the last note had been sung and they had stopped sobbing did Hoss interrupt them. He offered Grandma Spider a cigarette.

"What the fuck are you?" she blurted out, which sent her two companions into fits of laughter.

"What?" asked Hoss, unsure of what he should say.

"Injun, Chicano, Chinese? What the hell are you, boy?"

"I'm Native."

"Well, whatcha got there?"

"A Newport."

"I don't smoke menthols. What do I look like, a criminal?" asked Grandma Spider. On six spindly legs she stepped back. Her shriveled brown face and gray hair disappeared into shadow, but the wrinkles on her face were mirrorlike and glowed, reflecting moonbeams of decades and centuries past.

"No, Grandma. Sorry," apologized Hoss, slipping the Newports back into his pocket.

"What do you want? Searching for answers, I presume?"

"Yeah. I was kinda wanting to know how I can become a warrior."

The on-call warriors laughed again, but this time Grandma Spider shut them up. Then she motioned for them to leave. When they were gone, Grandma Spider circled Hoss, her legs stabbing at the concrete. She looked him up and down and all around. Hoss began to sweat. It wasn't the fact that she had the torso of an old Indian woman and the legs of a spider that intimidated him. No, it was her wisdom. It was great.

"What's your name?" Grandma Spider snarled.

"Rodney Dunree," he answered softly.

"So, how old are you, Rodney Dunree?"

"Eighteen."

"And you want to be a warrior?"

"Yes, Grandma, so I can fight for my people."

"Where's your hair at, boy?"

"I can grow it out if I have to."

"Your nose—too pudgy. Doesn't look like an Indian nose to me! But we can get around that. I'll take you to one of those fancy Hollywood doctors and we'll straighten it up for you."

"I'll do whatever is necessary, Grandma."

"How many horses do you have?"

"Only one, but it's a good one. We call it Silver."

"Got any weapons to strike down your enemy with?" she spit.

"I got a couple pistols, a few blades, but I like to use a weapon not too many Natives know how to use these days—my mind."

"How do you use that one?"

"I survive when they don't want me to."

"Have you ever killed any of your enemies?"

". . . yeah."

"Did you get a scalp?"

"No, didn't get the chance. We were driving by too fast. But I did get a fierce reputation."

"Huh! Well, how's your reputation for hunting? Can you hunt?"

"Let me see. I'm a mean beaver hunter," joked Hoss, but Grandma Spider didn't care for his little joke. Charm was not on his side.

"Funnyman, huh? I bet you couldn't tell me a good joke in your own tongue, could you?"

"No, Grandma."

"That's what I thought. What about a vision quest? Been on one yet?"

"There was this one time, me and my homeboy took some 'shrooms. When I started to throw up, worms came out of my mouth. Then everything started to turn into worms—my fingers, my arms, even my homeboy. It was freaky."

"So, you must be from the worm clan!" She laughed.

"There's a worm clan?"

"Now there is." She laughed even more. Hoss didn't like it.

"Okay, I've never been on a vision quest, then."

"What about an Indian name?"

"All I got is my street name. It's Hoss."

"What about your teepee?"

"Just like everyone else's brick teepee around here; three bedrooms, one bath, and a single-car garage."

"And wives?"

"I wouldn't call her my wife, but I got this one girl who comes over to my house a lot. Her name is Every-Rose-Has-Its-Thorns. But everybody calls her Rose."

"Can she cook good fry bread?"

"Doesn't have to 'cause I know where they have all the good Indian taco sales."

"And clan. Which clan does she come from?"

"The ram; she is an Aries."

"Aries, my ass! Well, do you at least know who the last great chief was?"

"That's an easy one—Marcus Allen."

"Who?"

"Marcus Allen. You know, he played for the Comancheville Chiefs."

"You got to be fuckin' kidding. Ah, never mind that. One last thing. Let me hear your war cry."

"Right here? Right now?"

"No, I want you to come back later. Of course, right now."

"Whooo wheee!" shouted Hoss at the top of his lungs.

"Okay! Okay! That's enough! That is enough!" screamed Grandma Spider with her hands over her ears.

Hoss smiled, exposing his dimples. That shout had made him feel good. "So, what'd you think?" he asked.

"Were you, by chance, raised by apes?" she joked, sending herself into laughter.

"Yeah, they call me Tarzan," Hoss replied sarcastically.

Seeing his hurt, Grandma Spider stopped laughing and crawled closer to him. Her face revealed the news. "I'm sorry, Rodney, but you are still a brave. To fight for your people is to want to die for your people. You are not ready for death. Come back another time, when you are more ready, and I'll take another look at you."

The news hit Hoss hard, even though it was the answer he had expected. He left in shame, nothing more than a brave. Grandma Spider whistled, and her two companions emerged from a cold shadow. Another Ghost Dance song started. As its wishful melody filled the air, Hoss walked back to Silver, where Maddog and Tricky were waiting for him anxiously. He climbed into the car.

"Damn, Kemosabe. 'Bout time. So, you a warrior or what?" asked Maddog.

"Fuck it," Hoss answered. It was clear he was pissed.

When Hoss lost his temper, it was never good. For a little guy, he could cause all kinds of ruckus. "What? Did she tell you no?" His best friend knew how to keep his boy's anger at bay.

"She said I was still just a brave. Believe that? A fuckin' brave." Hoss chewed on his bottom lip. It was how he calmed himself down.

"Y-you're still young," muttered Tricky, who reeked of mouthwash all of the sudden. "Y-you g-got a lot of t-time, *piah-phee*."

"Yeah, man. Why are you listening to Grandma Spider, anyways? All she knows is wine these days. Better off asking her what's best for dinner—red or white wine," joked Maddog. He made himself laugh.

Hoss smiled, too. "True, but it'd be nice to have her blessing as a warrior."

"Fuck that. The way I see it is you already are, man."

"Dog, you trippin'."

"Nah, for reals. Hell, we all are. We fight in battles

every day, and I mean every fuckin' day. It might not be like the battles in the old days, but the war is still on. And it's still us versus the white man. Check it out, though, but it's different these days because our enemy isn't even in human form anymore; he's in liquid form. On the reals. Hell, we got some liquid white man right here. This muthafucker calls himself Gin, but I know he's just a white man in disguise. And he's just sitting here, chillin' with us. Look at him. Hell, I think every Native battles the liquid white man at least once in his lifetime. But it's all the time for us.

"I'll tell you what, Hoss. I ain't letting the liquid white man get hold of me. Never. Fuck him! I got plans. Really. I'm gonna quit all this bullshit we do and take my ass to college and get me an education. And when I get my degree in my hand—I bullshit you not—I'm gonna laugh in the white man's face, then shoot him right between the fuckin' eyes. That'll show him that not even an education can change a true warrior! A soldier! Whooo! That's what I'm fuckin' talkin' about! Fuck 'em all!" shouted Maddog.

"You're crazy, dog," said Hoss, and he shook his head at his best friend, who sometimes understood him and sometimes didn't. Hoss started the car, pulled away from the nameless liquor store, and drove out of town, into the unknown, a.k.a. home.

The Storyteller
1996

"Fuck!" Mausape shouted. He got up from the rusted bunk bed and jumped to the cold cement floor below. He had been in the third tank of the NDN City jail for only one week, but already it felt like a year. Claustrophobia was starting to set in. Ten of them shared five small cells inside the tank, each cell barely big enough for a bunk bed and a toilet, and each cell equipped with barred doors that closed at sleeping time. At any other time, the doors were open so that the inmates could walk around in a larger room. The larger room wasn't large at all, just the equivalent of all five cells put together. Three tables were scattered around it, and the lights were always too bright. If anybody wanted to sleep during the day, he had to hang a sheet or blanket in front of his cell entrance. Almost every cell had a gleaming white sheet or a dingy green blanket covering its entrance. To make things worse, the color of the tank was the dullest of blues, almost hospital blue.

The only thing Mausape couldn't complain about was the company. All nine cellmates were X-Indians like himself. He was among his people. Even though he was just skin and bones, not to mention a little preppy, he didn't have to worry about anybody fucking with him. He was one of Brando's main men. *Brando* was the street name of his best friend, Marlon, who ran the drug business in NDN City. That gave Mausape a lot of pull on the inside.

Mausape took a seat in the only empty chair at the table where three of his cellmates were playing dominoes.

"Dang, Buckshot, you all right?" said Mike. Mike was chubby, dark, and always in high spirits. He brought life to their little home away from home, and he had given Mausape the nickname Buckshot a few days earlier. He gave everybody a nickname.

"I can't believe I'm still in here," complained Mausape. "Something's up. Brando should have bailed my ass out by now. And if he don't get me out soon, they'll never let me out."

"One of these days, you'll wake up and be out of this muthafucker," said Roderick, "but today's not the day." Roderick was almost too clean-cut to be in jail. He had a Noxema-washed face and nicely shaven head. And he had a certain air to him, almost as if he didn't mind being in there at all.

"No one can bail you out until you go to court first, bops. That's why they've been delaying your court date," explained Richard, the oldest inmate. "They're trying to keep you in here as long as they can. Come on, *piah-phee,* you know they ain't going to let someone busted with twenty pounds of weed and a kilo of coke walk out of here just like that. First they're going to want to know where it came from and where it was going." Richard was twenty-two, with long, dusty brown hair. He was a pretty mellow cat, liked to play the guitar, or so he said.

"They can keep me in here as long as they want, then," Mausape replied. "I ain't telling them shit."

"I wish we had some of that weed right now," said Roderick.

"You're tellin' me. Fuck the *mah-zanes,* Buckshot! Fuckin' pigs!" Mike yelled, slamming his last domino on the table. He hated the police with a passion.

"I'll find a way out somehow. For reals. Hey, let me jump in y'alls' game."

"Was that it?" Richard asked Mike. "Domino?"

"What do you think? Hey, Buckshot, tell us one of your crazy-ass stories," Mike said. A Mausape story was the pinnacle of Mike's day.

"Yeah, let's hear a good one, brother," said Richard.

"It's too early. Ah, fuck it. I guess I can tell y'all one I came up with not too long ago. It's like a traditional story, but with, you know, my twist on it."

"Traditional? Like pow-wows and shit?" asked Roderick.

"Nah. It's about this old mythical character named Saynday my grandpa used to tell me about. He's my tribe's hero, so we got all these stories about him doing all kinds of heroic shit, but the outcome always ends up teaching you something. Y'all know what I mean?"

"Yeah," they said.

"All right, here's the weird thing about this Saynday character, though. You see, he was a coyote and he was a trickster. And for as long as I can remember, I have always wanted to write my own Saynday story from my own imagination. Well, a few months back, I was sitting with my grandma and she told me all of the stories again, in the order they're supposed to be told. You see, these stories are so sacred that they have to be told in order. And one more thing— they're supposed to be told only in the wintertime."

"What kind of shit is that?" asked Roderick.

"Hell if I know. But anyways, in the last story, Saynday sees that the Kiowas are doing well, so he leaves, never to be seen again, and his whereabouts are forever after unknown. So I invented the story of his return and death. A summer story, I guess. It'll probably end up of-fending a lot of my people, but fuck 'em. I just wanted to test my storytelling ability."

"Yeah, fuck 'em," Mike said. "If you got some sto-ries, Buckshot, tell 'em."

"All right, here it goes, then. This one is called 'Saynday's Losing Battle.' Oh, yeah, I forgot to tell y'all. Every Saynday story starts the same, just like this. . . .

"Saynday was coming along, one day. He was going to check on his people, the Kiowas, because he hadn't seen them in a whole century and he wanted to make sure they were doing well. You see, the white man had just started to invade the Indian Territory, so Saynday wanted to make sure his people weren't in any trouble with them. When he arrived at his peoples' land, he stopped at a crossroads called the Apache Y. There were three roads and each one led to different villages of the Kiowas. One road led to NDN City, one to Kiowaton, and the last one to Apacheapolis. Saynday didn't know which Kiowas he should visit first, so he decided to rest and think about it. They had grown in great numbers since he'd seen them last.

"As soon as he took a seat in some buffalo grass, an owl appeared on a fence post nearby. It screeched, 'Saynday and the Kiowas! Saynday and the Kiowas!'

At first, Saynday pretended not to hear it. He knew that when an owl calls your name, it is a sure sign of death. The owl wouldn't stop, though, so Saynday grabbed his bow, and before the owl could hoot another syllable, Saynday yelled, 'Owl! Owl!' and shot an arrow right through the owl's heart. By doing so, he countered the owl's curse. After the owl fell to the ground, Saynday ran up to it and asked who had sent it. The owl only replied, 'The Evil Spirit will have its revenge!' Then the owl burst into flames. Witchcraft.

"Now, Saynday knew the Evil Spirit very well because he had fought many battles against it and had beaten the Evil Spirit many times. Saynday had strong medicine. So he wasn't intimidated by the Evil Spirit in the least. In fact, he called out to the Evil Spirit, yelling, 'Evil one, where are you? I will fight you again. I will win again. My people and I do not fear you. Show yourself, coward! You will lie next to your messenger. You will lie dead. Show yourself, coward!' To Saynday's disappointment, nothing happened. But it didn't surprise Saynday because he knew the Evil Spirit feared him.

"But then, magically, from out of the ground appeared four unique bottles: a bottle of liquor, a bottle of beer, a bottle of whiskey, and a bottle of wine. At the time, Saynday didn't know what they were. He just assumed that they were a peace offering from the

Evil Spirit. So he picked up all four of the bottles and shouted, 'You will not face me! But I will accept the peace offerings you make in your cowardness!'

"Soon Saynday was on his way again. But halfway to Kiowaton, he grew thirsty and decided to take a drink from one of the bottles. One drink led to another, and another, yet the bottle always remained full. Witchcraft, but good witchcraft. Each drink Saynday took made him feel better than the one before. That made him want to share the good-feeling medicine with his people.

"When Saynday arrived in Kiowaton, his people fell in love with the good-feeling medicine. In village after village, all of his people fell in love with the good-feeling medicine. Saynday decided to leave a bottle at each village but kept one for himself.

"It didn't take long for Saynday to notice what the good-feeling medicine was doing to his people. Men were cheating on their wives, beating on them, and skipping out on them. The women were going astray, too. They began to take many different partners, which left many children fatherless. And they stopped doing their duties as women altogether.

"Saynday could now sense evil in the good-feeling medicine. He knew he had to get it away from his people, but not even he could give it up. He was hooked. They were all deteriorating because of their thirst for the good-feeling medicine. It was really pathetic. They became the first Indian alcoholics.

"Saynday came to realize that the bottles weren't peace offerings at all but the Evil Spirit himself in disguise! Saynday had been in a battle with the Evil Spirit and didn't even know it, and the Evil Spirit was close to defeating him. Saynday wasn't about to let that happen. With all his strength and willpower, he broke free from the bonds of the good-feeling medicine, gathered all of the bottles together, and destroyed them. It was probably the most heroic thing he ever did.

"Saynday claimed victory again, or so he thought. What he didn't know was that his people had already found a new source for the good-feeling medicine. White men brought the good-feeling medicine to the I.T. by the barrel. The thirst of Saynday's people grew worse.

"Now, Saynday wasn't just going to stand by and watch his people destroy themselves, so he devised a plan. He would show them the kind of damage the good-feeling medicine was inflicting on them. To prove his point, he sacrificed himself. He started drinking the good-feeling medicine as much as possible, letting his people see it take him under. It grew utterly disgusting. He pissed on himself and passed out in public places. His health was gone. And in a short time, Saynday drank himself to death. But his fatal example didn't work. Worse, it influenced a whole generation to follow his example—a slow suicide in a stolen world.

"To the Kiowas, Saynday's death was just another wino passing on. It didn't hold the significance it should've. They did, at least, give him a decent burial. They buried him dead in the center of their land, out at the Apache Y, where the four bottles had first appeared. Even to this day, when you drive through the Apache Y, you can look toward the southeast and see a small hill. That is where Saynday is buried: in the heart of Kiowa country, where he lost his first battle and his last. And that's how it was, and that's how it is, to this good day."

"So you killed him? Damn you, Buckshot," said Mike.

"Damn, *piah-phee,* that was a good one," said Richard. "The best Saynday story I've ever heard."

"You need to write that down and sell it," added Roderick. "You could make a million dollars just like that."

"Ramrod's right. You ever think about that, Buckshot?" Mike asked. "Being a big-time Native writer?"

"You mean like Sean Arrows?" Mausape said.

"Who?" asked Mike. None of them knew the name.

"Never mind. Actually, I've been trying to get some

■ 78 ■

of my writing published, but being stuck here in NDN City, it's just not happening, man."

"Hell, yeah, they not trying to see a Native succeed around here. What'cha gotta do, Buckshot, is get the hell out of Dodge," Mike said. "And I'm not just talking about jail, but out of NDN City. Hell, out of the I.T., if you can."

"He's right," Richard agreed.

"That's what I'm screaming," said Roderick.

"But it's easier said than done," Mausape concluded. "Who's mixing 'em?"

They started a fresh game of dominoes.

Two days later, Mausape was sitting at a plain table in a small empty room. There were no windows, only a mirror. He had been waiting for twenty minutes and was becoming impatient. He needed a cigarette. Finally, the door opened and a familiar face entered the room. Mausape knew that what he was about to do was either going to be the worst thing he had ever done or the best.

"Hello, Mausape," said Deco, an NDN City police officer. "Find everything okay?" Mausape had had countless run-ins with the tall, pale coward before. Deco was a thorn in his side, but a thorn he knew well.

Under normal circumstances, he hated Deco, but at the moment, Deco was his savior, his knight in shining armor. "I'll be doing a lot better when I get out of here," Mausape answered.

"Well, that's what we're here to talk about, right? How fast we can get you out of this situation you've gotten yourself into. This very bad situation."

"Do you have a cigarette?"

"It's not a menthol, but here." Deco pulled out a pack of Winstons and threw one at Mausape. Cowboy-cigarette-smoking muthafucker. He had been watching Brando's crew for some time now, long enough to know they all loved menthol cigarettes.

"It's bad luck to throw tobacco. Can you hand me another one?"

"Didn't know you was superstitious, Mausape." Deco handed Mausape another cigarette and even lit it for him. Mausape took a long, ceremonial puff, then exhaled into Deco's face.

"So . . . did you get hold of the judge?"

"Sure did, and he approved everything."

"So after I make this statement and testify against Brando, you guys will relocate me and my wife through the Witness Protection Program?"

"That's the deal, but we want testimony of everything that Brando has been a part of: drugs, assaults, burglaries, car thefts, murders—everything."

"As long as you guys keep your end of the bargain, I'll keep mine."

"You're a good man, Mausape. You'll be doing NDN City a huge favor. But just between you and me, what made you want to be so cooperative all of the sudden?"

"Change."

"Change?"

"Yeah, change. I think it's time for me to broaden my horizons, see what else is out there for me. Maybe I'll write a book or something."

"Write a book? About what, dealing drugs? Well, whatever it was, I'm glad you finally came to your senses."

"Let's just get it over with."

"Fine with me; let's get started, then. Right now all we are going to do is get a recorded confession from you. Just explain how you came to know Brando, how everything started, the dealings you two had and all of the people involved. We need details, so be as specific as you can."

"Aren't you going to record this?"

"We've been recording. You can't see it, but there's a shotgun mic fixed on you. Now let's get this under way. You ready? All right, here we go. My name is Officer Deco Smith and it is July 10, 1996. I am here with Mausape Onthaw, who has agreed to have his statement recorded for use in a court of law against Marlon Buffalo, a.k.a. Brando, who is the leader of a drug cartel stationed here in NDN City. Okay, Mausape, your turn."

"I'd like to start from the beginning, if you don't mind," Mausape said.

"Go ahead."

Mausape thought about how he should begin, but there was only one way.

"Marlon was coming along one day. . . ."

A Vitamin-A Vision Quest
1999

It was Memorial Day weekend and Marlon couldn't remember a thing. It had been one of them nights for him and his roommate, Randy. For a pair of twenty-two-year-old X-Indian bachelors going to college in the White Man's Territory, short-term amnesia occurred more than frequently. On this particular morning, though, Marlon suffered from it worse than usual. He couldn't remember a single detail from the previous night.

Rum dumb as hell, he crawled out of bed and walked out onto the deck of his apartment. Like he always did on those mornings, he pissed off the deck and observed the clouds for a sign of something, anything. The clouds said that they were bringing weird weather but brought no answer to the question of who he had fucked the night before. He knew he had fucked someone, because there was an assortment of empty condom packets on his bedroom floor. Not to mention a naked woman in his bed. It didn't worry Marlon all that much, though. It happened all the time. Women adored him. He was quite the catch: nice-looking, smart, ambitious, and just this close to becoming a lawyer. To tell the truth, not knowing who he fucked didn't bother him at all. Knowing was sometimes worse.

After relieving himself, he walked back into the messy apartment. The television was still on, and a video on MTV looked worth watching. Marlon took a seat on his couch. Then Randy emerged from his bedroom with his snag of the night before. The sun blinded them. Yes, it must have been one of them nights.

"Damn, you still up, or you just getting up?" Randy asked, rubbing his bulky stomach. He had a build like Marlon's. Together, they were large and in charge, both equipped with book smarts and street smarts. They were actually from the same area in the I.T., too, but had never met back home. Randy was from Comancheville, which was quite a drive from NDN City. It was crazy, though, because Randy was also an ex–drug dealer trying to do good. And his old connection just so happened to be Marlon's old connection, Jabba, the fat-ass Mexican. Small world.

"Just getting up, fool," Marlon answered. His voice was deep and raspy, as it always was.

"Where's Wendy? She take off?"

"Wendy?"

"Yeah. Remember? You brought her home from the club last night."

"Oh, Wendy. She's still crashed out."

"Well, I'm taking Autumn home. If Wendy needs a ride, tell her now's the time."

"Let me go check," Marlon said.

Before he entered his room, Marlon combed his long hair with his fingers. It was unbraided, which was probably Wendy's doing. He was also wearing nothing but his boxers. He ate a lot, but he worked out a lot, too, and the delicate balancing of it all was very impressive to women. He was a hunk, a great big chunk of pure X-Indianness. As soon as Marlon opened his bedroom door, there she was—Wendy McMoy, a beautiful Caucasian woman with long blond hair and a pair of long legs to match. She was in the middle of pulling her rose-colored panties up over her tanned legs and untanned pelvic area. He loved tan lines. And he especially loved every curve of Wendy's womanly body. She was fleshy in just the right places and with just the right thickness, almost an X-Indian woman's thickness. He snuck a few glances as she walked around the room, searching for the rest of her clothes, not even a little ashamed of the stretch marks childbearing had left her with. She was a beautiful single mother and an occasional snag of Marlon's.

"Last night was on, huh?" Marlon finally said, just because it gave him a reason to be looking at her while her breasts were still uncovered. Her breasts weren't tanned, either. Damn, he loved tan lines!

"From what I could remember of it," she answered, combing her hair with Marlon's brush. That was when a memory hit him, a flashback. They were both on the floor, on their knees, next to his bed. She was leaned up against the bed as he penetrated her from behind. All the while, she was stroking the back of his head with one of her hands. There was an R. Kelly CD playing in the background.

"Did you hear Randy?" Marlon asked, forcing himself to return to the present.

"Yeah, tell him I'm almost ready. Damn, I still got to go get my son from his dad and then take him to my mom's so I can go to work. Uh, I'm going to be late again."

"J. C. Penney's open on Memorial Day weekend?"

"Hell, yeah. Got this damn sale going on."

"Let's go!" yelled Randy from the front room. Marlon looked at Wendy. He tried to tell her "I'm sorry I can't commit myself to you," but she seemed to read it in his eyes and lightly touched his arm as though to say it was okay.

"Well, I got to go. Call me sometime," she said.

As soon as Marlon heard Randy's car drive off, he jumped into the shower, got semidressed, and waited on the deck for his roomie's return. They had to get something going, just because it was a holiday.

Marlon surveyed the weird weather again. It was a good day to die. He thought about drinking a beer, but while he was arguing with himself over what the consequences would be, Randy pulled up in his dark green Camaro Z28 and parked. He honked for no apparent reason, or maybe because he could hear Marlon arguing with himself.

One of their downstairs neighbors, their skinhead buddy Fritz, followed Randy up to the deck. Fritz had on his usual military gear.

"What's going on, Marlon?" Fritz asked. He was just a skinny, bald-headed white boy with an ugly goatee. His bald head reminded Marlon of two of his best friends back in NDN City. But they wouldn't have called Marlon by his real name. No. They would've called him by his street name, Brando.

"Not a damn thing. What about you?" he asked back, out of courtesy.

Randy said, "Fritz was just telling me he got hold of some good acid."

"No shit, Fritz. You going to hook us up or what?" Marlon asked.

"Yeah, I got some, if you're interested."

"What do you think, Marlon?" Randy asked. "It's Saturday, we ain't got shit to do, and we don't have to work until Tuesday. Feel like taking a journey?"

Randy scratched his head through his short, tangled

hair. He always did that when he was trying to talk Marlon into doing something.

"A motionless journey . . . ?" Marlon said, considering it.

"Come on, Marlon. I know you ain't scared. I'll tell you what: I'll sell you some at friend prices. Seven dollars a hit," offered Fritz, smiling suspiciously, but then again, he was probably tripping, and maybe he wanted to share his joy with the world.

"What do you think, Marlon?" Marlon could tell that Randy's mind was already made up. He just didn't like to do things alone.

"Fuck it!" Marlon declared, deciding. "I really do need to go on a vision quest. What'cha got, Fritz?"

"I got some shit straight from the Third Reich. Some Adolf Hitler shit," he answered, and pulled out a white tab that was half an inch by half an inch, with a swastika on it.

"Damn, that looks like some evil shit," Marlon said. He meant "evil" as in "good." Most good acid had something printed on it, which meant the maker was proud of his work.

"Fuck it, give me two hits," said Randy, and Fritz pulled out two tabs from a small crack-cocaine bag.

"I'll take two, too."

"A wise decision, my friends," said Fritz, "because I don't know how long I will have this shit, and you know

I like to help friends out first. Cool. Nice doing business with you. I'm going back in. Oh, yeah. Remember— stick to the road and watch the moon," he joked, and walked back downstairs, counting the twenty-eight dollars they had given him.

"Here goes nothin'," announced Randy, and he put the two tabs under his tongue.

"Well, here I go. 'Bout to get my vision quest on," Marlon said, and did the same.

"Hey, let's go get some movies to trip out on."

"Hell, yeah. Probably got some time before this shit hits us, anyways."

Marlon and Randy jumped into Randy's mean green machine and drove to a neighborhood video store. Choosing the movies became a vision quest in and of itself. It always happened that way with them. They would walk around until one chose them. Some days they were Chief Austin Powers and other days they would be Chief Titanic. Finally, after an hour had passed, Marlon and Randy agreed on two movies: *Meet Wally Sparks*, with Rodney Dangerfield, and *The Long Kiss Goodnight,* with Samuel L. Jackson and Geena Davis. They split the bill, then made their way home at a slow and eerie pace. The weather was starting to get even weirder.

The clock read 3:10 p.m. by the time Randy slapped *Wally Sparks* in. The movie had its funny moments, but in the end, they both gave it two thumbs down.

"Feeling anything yet?" asked Randy. He sounded normal.

"Nah, what about you?" Marlon asked back. But Marlon *did* feel something, a kind of uplifting feeling, extremely light. "Slap in the next one," he said.

"Fuck it," Randy said as he put in *The Long Kiss Goodnight*. It was an action movie with a cool plot.

They sat on the edges of their seats as they watched the most spectacular movie they'd ever seen in their lives! They were thrown into the action immediately. They dodged bullets. They shielded themselves from shrapnel. And every explosion was so loud, it made them hold their ears. It became a freakin' war in that living room, and Marlon and Randy feared for their lives. Everything was loud, ludicrously bright, and unreal.

When the movie ended, Marlon and Randy just sat in bewildered silence, expecting the unexpected. Marlon could actually feel his reality bending and shape-shifting out of control, his mind like an ocean with waves of thoughts. Everything seemed to have so much meaning to him, everything from the half-smoked cigarette in his ashtray to the pool of television static he and Randy were floating on. Only one word came to mind—"trippy." Then, suddenly, he felt closed in, like he couldn't breathe. He panicked and fled outside to get some air.

Out on the deck, Marlon started hallucinating more. The weather was flat-out crazy now. The clouds were melting and the wind carried in sounds from afar. Marlon could hear an elephant, a galloping horse, a clown laughing, and a loud bumblebee buzzing somewhere nearby. Then he saw something green come at him from out of nowhere. But it was just Randy with his Columbus City Explorers hat on; they were Randy's favorite football team.

"I'm fuckin' trippin', for reals," admitted Marlon. They both stared up at the clouds. The clouds were very entertaining, melting the way they were.

"Makes you wonder," Randy finally said.

"About what?"

"If it's the fuckin' end of the world."

They both busted out laughing. And they laughed and laughed. Then they laughed some more. It was good to be alive.

When the laughter finally gave way to words, Marlon and Randy talked a hundred miles per hour. They talked about anything and everything they could think of. UFOs, Bigfoot, and the Loch Ness monster intrigued their philosophical minds. Arguments about which came first, the chicken or the egg, put the two scholars to the test. Before they knew it, the sky had reached them, and, drop by drop, it began to fall.

It took Marlon and Randy a lot longer than it should've to realize that it was raining pretty hard and that they were soaking wet.

"This is fucked up," Marlon said with perfect timing. And they both busted out laughing again. Realizing that they looked like two crazy muthafuckers laughing in the rain, Marlon and Randy ran back inside.

"Let's go do something, Ran," Marlon said.

"Hell, yeah. I was about to say the same thing," Randy answered.

"Feel like playing some pool?"

"Don't matter to me! Balls? Or what?"

"Balls sounds good!"

After Marlon and Randy had cleaned up, they hopped into Randy's green Knight Rider–like car. They had to do something to keep their minds occupied; they were both still in the hallucination stage of their acid trip. The good news was that the acid was mellowing them out now, the weird weather was gone now.

It took forever for them to drive to Balls, a local pool hall. Streetlights along the way glowed and shot out the most beautiful colors, colors Marlon had never seen before, like purple-green, orange-turquoise, and a blackish yellow. One word came to mind—"groovy."

They arrived at Balls like bats out of hell. It was a two-story brick building full of pool tables and rock 'n' roll music, a common hangout for Indians and X-Indians alike. A very rare place in the W.M.T., where very few of their kind dwelled. Marlon and Randy were inside before they even remembered getting out of the car. Right away, their friend Dio greeted them from his table: "What are you two knuckleheads up to?" Dio was a giant of an X-Indian, even bigger than Marlon and Randy. He was six feet six inches tall and carried three hundred pounds of the purest ruggedness.

"Just come to swim some pool," Marlon replied, fucking up. He turned to Randy, and they broke up laughing.

"Anyways, what about you, man?" Randy asked Dio.

"I'm trying to get out of town for a while."

"Where to?" Marlon asked.

"Trying to go to Columbus City."

"Columbus City? What for?" Randy asked, like he cared.

"To party at the District. I got a little fundage; my lease check came in today. What do you think?" Dio asked. "You game?"

"You put some gas in my car, get me and Marlon into wherever we go, and I'm game," Randy answered. He was scanning the terrain for any prey. Not a victim in sight.

"I got this chick with me, though. Is it cool if she rolls?" Dio asked with a look that said "Don't even think about cockblockin' my ass."

"It's your money. So when do you wanna leave?"

"The sooner the better. I'll go get her."

Dio walked four pool tables down and led an intoxi-cated X-Indian chick, one they all knew, back toward them. Together, the four exited the bar.

They drove to the George Washington Turnpike and began their thirty-minute trip from College Park to Columbus City. On the way, Marlon fixated on another trip, a trip during which he might possibly find something of great importance—himself. All of the business about this new trip, to Columbus City, had stalled what he be-lieved was his vision quest. He gathered his thoughts back together and felt the effects once again. It was a good feeling.

Halfway there, they stopped at a turnpike gas station located in the middle of nowhere and gassed up. While they were parked, Marlon stared out of his window at the moonlit plains laid out before them. Across the highway, he spotted a group of teepees, authentic and faded. Not like the ones at pow-wows, which were colorful and clean. Suddenly, out of nowhere, Indian women began to appear near the teepees, taking care of daily chores and other tasks. They were real Indian women, not like the X-Indian women Marlon had grown up with. One word came to mind—"uncivilized." His concentration on a few sexy, authentic beauties bent over, gathering berries, was broken by three horsemen approaching the camp. There was an Afro-American man, a Caucasian man, and a Mexican man. The three charged into the camp and with utmost ease captured all of the Indian women. Marlon watched in disbelief, all the while wondering where the Indian men were.

Shortly after the raid, the three horsemen rode off with all of the Indian women as their captives, treating them as if they were a herd of cattle. They were all so helpless. Marlon began to wonder if he should run to their rescue or at least say something. But then he remembered something else, something important: he was trippin'. He had totally forgotten this and didn't remember until Randy slammed his door shut. Oh, was he trippin'! Regardless, he thought about what he had just seen and wondered if it had anything to do with his vision quest. Maybe it did; maybe it didn't. Or was it just some weird episode of the acid trip, brought on by Marlon's expectation of seeing an animal whose name he could claim as his new X-Indian name?

"Damn, I'm trippin'," he said out loud.

"Hell, yeah, me too. I don't know how long I was in that mug. Felt like fuckin' forever, though," admitted Randy. Then he drove off and sped back onto the highway. Within seconds, his speedometer read ninety-five miles per hour. Marlon couldn't stand it when Randy drove that fast. For comfort, he turned and looked at Dio and the intoxicated X-Indian chick, Dio's very own barrel full of monkeys.

"Y'all up?" he asked.

"Yeah, just jamming out," Dio answered while a Korn cassette played in the background. It was the *Life Is Peachy* album.

"We almost there yet? I wanna get my dance on," said the intoxicated X-Indian chick, moving her small breasts to the hard guitar riffs.

"Not too far to go," Randy said comfortingly.

Marlon banged on the ceiling of the car two times, a gesture that meant he needed another beer. Dio handed him a nice cold Brewer's. Marlon killed half of it in one shot before going back to gazing at the road ahead of them. One word came to mind—"ahhh."

All of the sudden, out of nowhere, a figure appeared in the middle of the road. They were approaching it at a crazy speed, but the figure did nothing to get out of their way.

"Watch out!" Marlon yelled. Randy barely missed it.

Something strange had happened, though. As they were passing, time slowed, and Marlon could clearly see that the figure was a man, a strange-looking man wearing a long dark trench coat. Marlon's eyes met his, and a chill went up his spine. He even lost his breath. Everything grew silent for them few moments that they passed him. Then, in an instant, everything was back to normal, like nothing had happened.

"You all right?" Randy asked.

"Yeah, I'm cool, just—"

"Hey, I saw it, too," interrupted the intoxicated X-Indian chick. "It was, like, this big shadow man."

"Shut up, girl," Dio said, laughing her off.

"No. You shut up," she snapped. And as they argued, Marlon fell back into silence and drank his beer.

Another beer later, they were in Columbus City, making their way to the District—eight square blocks of bars, clubs, and liquor stores. Once in the District, they pushed through the street party that went down there every weekend. Marlon was still preoccupied with his episode at the gas station, and with the man in the road.

The group entered a two-story bar called Bunker Blues. It was a white-boy bar that had a deck wrapped around the upper half, where patrons could drink outside and view the District, with its mix of different-colored drunks. And the decks were happening. Dio ordered a round of fancy drinks, and they all stood against the deck railing. Just below them, standing on the other side of a small alley, was a small white guy playing familiar tunes on his acoustic guitar, his case open on the ground beside him so that people could throw in change. For a few dollars, he'd play any song requested. Or so the sign next to him said.

From above, Marlon watched a beautiful X-Indian woman walk over and place two dollars carefully in the case. She whispered into the guitarist's ear, then retreated into the bar. Marlon was jealous. He wished it could've been his ear. But before he lost sight of her, she threw him a small glance. He smiled at her.

"You know her?" asked Randy.

"Nah, never seen her."

"You better go push some game on her, for reals. If you don't, I will. Not too many Native chicks around here, you feel me?"

"How do y'all know she's Native? She could be Mexican or something, you know," said the intoxicated X-Indian chick, who had an empty glass in her hand that was filled with a Hurricane just minutes before.

"Oh, we know," said Dio, taking a sip of his Long Island iced tea. "It's a sense we have."

The musician ended one song and started another, which had to be the song the beautiful X-Indian woman had requested. It was a hard-rock tune. Marlon recognized the song but couldn't put a name on it. It was on the tip of his tongue. Then it hit him. Of course. It was "Man in the Box" by Alice in Chains. It was a good call, and after Marlon listened for a while, he found some meaning in its words. It expressed how he felt right then, like he was a boy trapped in a man's body, the man in him not quite arrived yet. The truth was, he felt he was the furthest he had ever been from being a man. He had a child back in NDN City, a son, to be exact, who was being raised by the mother alone. Oh, how he missed them.

But he could never return home, never. Home was equal to jail, and jail was equal to nothing. And the last thing he wanted to do was nothing. But what was he doing now? Yeah, he was in college, but doing things unworthy of manhood there, and very close to nothing. Sometimes he thought he only stayed and went to school in College Park because he was safe from his past there. He couldn't be extradited to the I.T. from the W.M.T.

After the song finished and he snapped out of his trance, Marlon went back to mingling with Randy and forgot all about those thoughts. His brain needed to get back on track again.

Five Captain Morgan and Cokes and eight beers later, all Marlon could hear was the guitar man's singing. It began to get on his nerves. His sense of hearing was turning on him. He had to do something, so he got two dollars' worth of quarters at the bar and, without warning, started chucking quarters at the guitar man. He threw his hardest, too, and hit the poor guy just about every time. The singing halted. Marlon could be a really mean drunk.

"Hey, man!" yelled the guitar man, who looked a lot like Shaggy on the cartoon *Scooby-Doo*.

"Shut the fuck up!" Marlon yelled back. "You know that song?" He was the only one who found his joke funny, though. The acid had worn off, and the alcohol was kicking his rowdiness in.

Randy and Dio grabbed Marlon and managed to

escort him downstairs and out to the car without any problem. Only one word came to Marlon's mind—"lemmego." But being the friend he was, he didn't give them too hard a time when they made him get into Randy's green speed demon. After that, they were outta there.

"Damn Natives. Always got to tear it," said the intoxicated X-Indian chick, popping open a beer.

"Fuck that. Like you weren't fucking up," Marlon said, reversing the blame, as men do. "I saw you trying to get next to them black muthafuckers."

"Is that right?" asked Dio.

"Hell, no, they were just trying to buy me a drink," she said in her defense.

"Shit. Looked more to me like you were getting a little jungle fever," said Randy.

"Fuck y'all. What's the matter? Y'all scared I might go black and never come back to y'alls' small dicks?"

"Yeah, right. It's more like 'go black and nobody will want your polluted pussy back,'" joked Dio, and they all laughed, except for the intoxicated X-Indian chick. She kept her mouth shut then, as if admitting that she wasn't any competition for three X-Indian boys when it came to talking shit.

Back on the turnpike, they fell into silence, and Marlon went back to staring into space. He tried to put everything together and come up with some kind of purpose to his vision quest. Nothing came to his mind. He was rather disappointed in his trip, both trips.

"Boy, that guy was pissed at you, Marlon," Randy blurted out.

"Who?" Marlon asked.

"Guitarzan."

"Fuck that muthafucker. Singing off-key and shit."

"He was like, 'Hey, man! Hey, man!'" Randy said, mimicking him.

And, just like that, it all clicked into place. Marlon knew what his vision quest was all about. It was so obvious! His first vision, of a village being invaded, was a reflection of how other cultures were taking over their women while X-Indian men did nothing about it. The women went with the marauders, not because they wanted to, but because they didn't have a better choice. X-Indian men were at their all-time worst, and X-Indian women had finally grown tired of putting up with it. They didn't want to be taken for granted anymore. They were leaving.

The man in the middle of the road was the second sign. Marlon had heard of people going on a vision quest and seeing an animal. Whatever animal they'd seen became their clan. There was a bear clan, a wolf clan, a rabbit clan, a hawk clan, and so forth, and every clan had its purpose. The way things were going, it should've been no surprise that a new clan had formed—the man clan, a clan designed to help their culture survive. The man clan was now Marlon's clan.

The third and fourth signs were the man with the guitar and the beautiful X-Indian woman at Bunker Blues. The woman had come and gone like a dream and had requested a song that would help Marlon focus on what he had to do. And he couldn't believe he hadn't seen it. The song was "Man in the Box." That was what Marlon was—he wouldn't let himself become a man, because he enjoyed being a boy more. At the bar, the guitar man had yelled it out in plain English: "Hey, man!"

But there was one more sign. It was the intoxicated X-Indian chick. She was on the edge of leaving her X-Indian men and going elsewhere to find someone, anyone, to appreciate her. She was a strong and hopeful X-Indian woman. And even though she took a lot of shit from Marlon and every other X-Indian man she knew, she still hung around to satisfy them in the hope that at least one of them cared for her. Deep down, she knew they cared. Marlon believed they all cared for her, but they had a bad way of showing her, with their rude gestures and the way they mistreated her.

They were almost back in College Park when Marlon turned the music down to make an announcement.

"I'm not going to be Marlon the boy anymore!" he

declared, his tone serious. "From now on, I will be Marlon the man."

But they all laughed at this sudden outburst.

"You for reals?" Randy asked when he'd stopped laughing.

"Hell, yeah. I'm tired of all this bullshit."

"Damn, Marlon. You going to fuck a black chick or what?" joked Dio, but only Randy and Dio laughed.

"No. I mean a real man. A good man. Hell, by the time I'm dead, I'll be the definition of a man."

"But whose man are you going to be?" asked the intoxicated X-Indian chick.

"The woman I owe my life to, my son's momma. Her name is Two-Rivers-Flowing Together."

"Hell, yeah," said Randy. "You the man, Marlon. You the man."

"Yeah, you the man," Dio said from the backseat.

And thus, Marlon was.

Amen.

The Case of X-Indians v. Al Cohol
2001

"Please rise for the Honorable Great Spirit. In the case of *X-Indians v. Al Cohol,* Prosecutor Marlon Buffalo will be representing the X-Indians, and Defense Attorney Beelzebub will be representing Al Cohol.

"Prosecutor Buffalo, please approach the bench!" shouted the courtroom officer, who looked like every courtroom officer: old and white.

"Thank you, sir," said the prosecutor. "Today we are here for the trial of Mr. Cohol. My clients, the X-Indians, have determined through rigorous research and firsthand experience that he is, without a doubt, the one solely responsible for the massive number of murders, repeated rapes, and countless assaults committed among members of their race. Further, that he plays the leading role in a conspiracy to kill off their entire culture. And my clients seek the Damnation In Hell Forever penalty, plus punitive damages for their generation's pain and suffering." Prosecutor Buffalo was armed with a confident lawyerly appearance. Sporting a tailor-made suit, a pair of high-priced shoes, and a neatly trimmed haircut, he was no longer the Marlon of his teenage years. He'd given up his past along with his long hair. And it was obvious that he was on his way to becoming a rich, successful lawyer.

"I object, Your Honor!" interrupted the deep-voiced Defense Attorney Beelzebub, the greatest demon of them all. "It is far too inappropriate to suggest any form of sentencing before my client has had a chance to prove his innocence." DA Beelzebub was fire red, and tall, with horns curling down from his head toward his chin. He was majestic in an evil sense, not ugly. His goat legs, however, were hideous, and he made the courtroom smell of sulfur.

"Objection sustained," ordered the Honorable Great Spirit, who was nothing but a light, yet a light so indescribably beautiful it could only be seen in the Courtroom of Humanity.

"Forgive me, Your Honor," said Prosecutor Buffalo. "I meant it only as a motion. Now, if there are no other objections, I'd like to proceed with the examination of my first witness. Mr. Cohol, please approach the witness stand."

Al Cohol, a demon who resembled a spiritlike ser-
pent, slithered his way up to the witness stand. Puffs of
smoke shot out of his body, creating a thin cloud around
him. A thicker haze hid his face, and, even in the light of
the judge, no features were visible except for a pair of
glowing red eyes.

"Do you swear to tell the truth, the whole truth, and
nothing but the truth, so help you Great Spirit?" asked
the courtroom officer.

"Yesss," answered Mr. Cohol, his voice cold as death.

"Please be seated."

"Yesss, sssir." Mr. Cohol coiled himself up inside the
witness stand. Smoke no longer came out of his body.

"Your name is Al Cohol, correct?" asked Prosecutor
Buffalo, pacing back and forth, twirling his thumbs. He
was fresh out of college and not very experienced in cases
like this: mythical, but priorities of humanity.

"Correct."

"And exactly when were you first introduced to my
clients' ancestors, the Indians?"

"Let me sssee. Fourteen hundred sssomething, fifteen
hundred sssomething. Sssomewhere around that time. I
don't recollect the exsssact date."

"Fine. But around that time, was there any sort of
conflict between you and the Indians?"

"No. Actually, we got along very well."

"Very well? As in, you tried to destroy them, the way

you are trying to destroy the X-Indians? Is that what you mean by 'very well'?"

"Objection!" shouted Defense Attorney Beelzebub, fire shooting from his mouth.

"Objection overruled," said the judge.

"I've never tried to dessstroy anybody," resumed Mr. Cohol, "essspecially them. They were friends of mine. My mossst loyal friends, I might add," he said slyly.

"So all of the pain and suffering was just a part of your 'friendship' with them? Well, my clients believe something entirely different. They believe that their ancestors were poisoned by you, that they were doing just fine until the day you came into their lives. Then it all went to hell—the hell you come from!"

"I thought thisss was about the X-Indians?"

"Oh, it is. Once you introduced yourself to the Indians years ago, your evil took root in them and has been passed down to my clients like some sort of diseased heirloom."

"Are you implying that I've been inherited by your clientsss?"

"I'm not implying anything. I'm telling it like it is. You put their ancestors in a hole they couldn't dig their way out of, which, in turn, put their children and their children's children in the very same hole. And you call yourself a friend. What kind of friend are you to them, exactly?" Prosecutor Buffalo asked.

"I've been there for them all, jussst as they have been

there for me," answered Mr. Cohol, fixing his gaze on the prosecutor as though he wanted to pierce his soul with his eyes.

"Is that so?"

"Actually, I'd consssider myssself more than jussst a friend to both the Indians and your clientsss. I'd like to think of myssself as more of a . . . father figure to them all."

"Interesting. Care to explain yourself?"

"Sure. As I recall, even you oncccе loved me as you would a father."

"I really doubt that, but please continue."

"Maybe I should ssstart from the beginning. As I recall, when I was firsssт introduced to the Indians, it was during a time when I had been around nothing but impurity. For centuries on end, I sssearched the world high and low to sssee if there was anyone left untainted. I wanted to be with people that were pure. I desssired it more than anything. That'sss when I came acrosss the Indians. Because they were ssso pure and untainted, I had to find a way into their bloodline ssso that I could forever be a part of them. Normally, this is an easy tasssk for a demon sssuch as myssself, but I musssт admit, with the Indians it wasn't as easy as anticipated. It took sssome time, but I eventually did manage to find a way into their way of life. And as sssoon as I was in, I made sure that I was there to ssstay. All it took was for me to coerce Indian men into impregnating Indian women, and thusss, my ssseed was planted.

My blood became their blood, and their blood became my blood. You sssee, your clientsss are gravely missstaken. I am not their adversssary; I am probably the only ancessstor they have left," explained Mr. Cohol, eyeing the Intertribal Council, which was seated behind the prosecutor.

"Well, I have to admit, that was a nice story, indeed. So what you're saying is, my clients owe their existence to you? Because we all owe our existence to our ancestors?"

"Yesss, very much sso. If it weren't for me, many of your clientsss would not have ever been conceived. I've even played a large part in raising mossst of them. Thusss, I mentioned being a father figure."

"Touching, but, believe me, that's far from the truth. How can you sit there and say you've been like a father to some of them?"

"On the contrary, Mr. Buffalo. You, esssecially, should undersssstand it."

"And I do. And it is a lie. But I'm sure everyone would like to hear what you have to say."

"Good, because you and I have sssuch a passst, Marlon.

"I was there when you were conceived; I made it happen.

"I was there bessside your mother, helping her raise you after your father left.

"I was the one who taught you how to fight, how to fornicate, and how to have fun.

"And when your ssson was conceived, I was there. I made it happen.

"And when you mourned the deathsss of your two friends, I held your hand.

"And when you look back at your life and you sssee only one ssset of footprintsss, that'sss because I carried—"

"I hate to interrupt such a creative destruction of the truth, but I think I speak for everyone when I say, let's move on, please."

"Sssorry if I have offended you."

"Don't worry, you didn't. But let me make one thing clear. You were the *reason* I lost my two best friends, and, I might add, probably the reason for thousands upon thousands of deaths in the X-Indian community. You are a murderer, and death is just one of the many problems you have caused for my clients. You are the main reason they lie, steal, and partake of other deviant wrongdoings that, in the end, cause problems with their families, their friends, and the law! Under your influence, they've become outcasts, criminals, and foes of anyone and everyone around them! Last, but not least, you prevent my people from doing anything positive for one another, which, ultimately, is destroying their culture! You need to be damned to the lowest pit of hell! You son of a bitch!"

"Objection! Objection, Your Honor!"

"Objection sustained. Mr. Buffalo, please show some self-control."

"Sorry." Prosecutor Buffalo took a breath, then continued. "Yes, my clients feel you are at fault for everything."

"And do you have proof of these accusationsss?" Mr. Cohol asked quickly. The question put a smile on the prosecutor's face.

"I thought you'd never ask. As a matter of fact, I do. They have been entered into the trial as Exhibit A. Both the judge and your attorney have been supplied with copies of the reports. There are literally millions of them. Now, to conclude my examination, I have just one more question for you. Why do you feel the need to inflict all of this pain and suffering upon my clients, the X-Indians?"

"There is no anssswer to your quessstion. I told you: I would never do anything to harm or hurt my people."

"They are not your people. You have no people. All you have is hate—hate for my people—and hate is forever lonely. It is obvious that you have no intention of answering my question, so I'm not going to waste any more of anyone's time. Besides, I have more than enough evidence to prove your guilt. That will be all, Your Honor." Prosecutor Buffalo returned to his seat and tried to calm himself. He was feeling it: he loved being a lawyer.

"You may return to your seat, Mr. Cohol," said the judge.

"I would now like to call on Defense Attorney Beelzebub to approach the bench!" shouted the courtroom officer.

"Thank you. I would like to start by calling on my first and only witness. Will the entire X-Indian race please approach the witness stand?" asked Defense Attorney Beelzebub. He was a rich red and barely had any clothing on at all. Very unprofessional.

"Objection! That's absurd. You can't call on the entire race," interrupted Prosecutor Buffalo.

"Objection sustained," said the judge.

"Then I will need a representative of their race to approach the stand."

"Prosecutor Buffalo, you will need to supply the defense with a representative of your clients' race," ordered the judge.

Something was up, and Prosecutor Buffalo could feel it. He loosened his necktie. He wasn't quite used to the tension yet, and going against the liar of all liars didn't help. Defense Attorney Beelzebub stood there, confident as ever. And the judge was not the least bit bothered by his presence. In fact, they started chatting together while Prosecutor Buffalo consulted with the Intertribal Council, whose members had gathered around him. After a long discussion, they agreed that Prosecutor Buffalo was best suited to represent them all.

"We have come to a decision," announced Prosecutor Buffalo. "I will represent my race, Your Honor." He was in over his head and knew it, but what choice did he have?

"Please approach the witness stand, Mr. Buffalo," the

defense attorney said. Marlon Buffalo approached the stand, but as an X-Indian, not a lawyer.

"Do you swear to tell the truth, the whole truth, and nothing but the truth, so help you Great Spirit?" asked the courtroom officer.

"Yes, sir," answered Marlon. The defense attorney approached with a gentleness that made Marlon feel oddly comfortable.

"Well, well, you've made some interesting points in the reports you supplied me with. They're interesting because it seems like every single one of them points the finger at my client as the cause for all of the crimes committed. But before we get to that, your name is Marlon Buffalo, originally from NDN City, right?"

"Correct."

"I love it there. Beautiful place. But now you reside here, in the White Man's Territory, right? What was it, exactly, that made you leave NDN City?"

"That's irrelevant to this case. Next question, please."

"You're right, it's not important. But let me ask you this. Have you ever interacted with my client before?"

"Yes. In the past I have."

"And exactly how long did you and my client interact? Once, twice? A year, two years?"

"I'm not sure."

"Would you say most of your life?" asked the defense attorney.

"Yes," Marlon reluctantly agreed, "but as for other X-Indians—"

"That's irrelevant. You are representing the entirety of your race here, so please refrain from any attempt to individualize yourself. It's safe to say you have an abundant knowledge about my client. Am I correct in saying so?"

"Yes."

"Then you must know that it is impossible for my client to manually or otherwise deliberately inflict any type of physical injury on a person? My client can influence a person's decision, but he does not have the form, ability, or capacity to control that person's actions, correct?" It was a question the whole courtroom tuned in to. One word popped into Marlon's mind—"checkmate."

"Yes, but," Marlon protested, "all the crimes I have in my reports were a direct result of his influence."

"But there was no gun to anyone's head. There was never any forceful threat made against your client by my client. Was there?"

Marlon didn't answer. There was silence.

"Were you or any other X-Indian ever *forced* to succumb to my client's influence?" the defense attorney continued.

After a lengthy pause, Marlon finally answered. "Could I have a moment to discuss this with the Intertribal Council?"

"Sure. Take all the time you need."

Marlon left the witness stand and calmly made his way over to the Intertribal Council. Whispers could be heard. A few members of the council even shouted as they discussed the question. The great thinkers of the tribes were being put to the test by the simple question. After hours of debate, they finally reached a decision. Marlon again took a seat at the witness stand.

"No, sir," answered Marlon. "Not necessarily." Marlon hated the answer, but it was the truth. The spectators started to murmur.

"That is all, Your Honor," concluded Defense Attorney Beelzebub, and he returned to the table where his client was happily seated. There was a grin on Mr. Cohol's face that made Marlon nervous.

Recess was called and, what felt like years later, the judge returned to the courtroom from his chambers. He had the verdict, the fate of one race. The X-Indians' welfare and future depended on the outcome of this trial. If Al Cohol didn't get convicted and sentenced, they were doomed. If he was allowed to maintain his evil grip on their race, they would never be able to move forward, never be able to make progress. Like many other races, they were helpless against Mr. Cohol. If he *did* get convicted and got the Damnation In Hell Forever penalty, then the X-Indians would receive a court-ordered freedom from his bondage. Chains would be broken; cycles would stop.

"Silence!" yelled the courtroom officer. "The judge has reached a verdict!" Silence quickly fell over the courtroom.

"I find the defendant, Al Cohol," announced Judge Great Spirit, "not guilty of any of the crimes for which he stands accused. He will be allowed to remain on Earth. As I have asked of other races in the past, I will now ask this of the plaintiffs: please deal with this issue among yourselves. My courtroom is not the place to seek help. This is something you must resolve on your own." Then Judge Great Spirit banged his gavel. Like thunder, it could be heard throughout the Indian Territory. Throughout the Indian Territory, all X-Indians were already drowning their sorrows in the company of their longtime companion, Al Cohol, as they had always done in the past and will always do in the future.

Twisted Owl Fear
1980

There was a belief shared by all Indians in the Indian Territory: owls were not to be fucked with. Owls had medicine—sometimes good, sometimes bad. And just about everyone had at least one owl story to tell. It might be the one about the man who heard an owl call his name and who then, two days later, died, or the one in which someone's aunt raced an owl down an old country road and beat it, then, a little while later, hit the jackpot at bingo. These were Indian urban legends at their best. But there was one legend that not too many people had heard. It was the one that involved Tricky, the one that told his tale, the one where he came to be what a lot of people considered "crazy." It happened many moons ago, in the dark year 1980, when Tricky was still known as Ron Reed, his birth name.

It was on the highway stretching from College Park to NDN City that this story began. Ron, who was just twenty-one at the time, couldn't have picked a more beautiful day for his long drive. The March warmth was all around, and the color green was beginning to invade the scenery again. Life was good, something Ron was getting quite used to. Even better was the reason for this particular trip. He was on his way to his hometown to see an old friend. It wasn't just any old friend, but his best friend, Thurman, better known as Swino. Ron and Swino made the most mismatched duo ever to live, seeing how Ron was a short curly-haired boy while Swino was tall and dark as ever. Hell, the only things the two had ever had in common were where they grew up and their race—Indian—which really didn't amount to a hill of beans; but it was enough for them.

It had been more than two years since they'd last crossed paths, and both were eager for this reunion. There were two main reasons they hadn't seen much of each other. The first was that Ron had gone off to the White Man's Territory to run track for the University of the White Man's Ways (UWMW). He was the fastest Indian in the hundred meter, two hundred meter, and four hundred meter, and in almost every other race. No one could beat him in the Indian Territory and, as he was finding out, no one in the White Man's Territory could, either. He was well on his way to the Olympics. Around the time Ron left for college, Swino got busted for dealing drugs and was sentenced to two years in the county jail. Swino's release date had finally arrived, and he was set to be a free man again at five o'clock on the dot that day. Ron wasn't going to miss it for the world.

Five o'clock hit and, sure enough, Ron was there to see Swino burst through the front doors of the county jail. After all that time behind bars, Swino was now almost as pale as Ron—almost-white—and he was wearing the biggest smile Ron had ever seen on his greasy face. Before saying a word, Swino ran up to the statue of Lady Justice, blind, as usual, and started to kiss it and run his hands up and down her ass. Ron laughed.

"I'm sorry, sugar," joked Swino, "but I gotta ramble on. I'm telling you, Ron, this was the only tail I had to look at for two years. I was having wet dreams like a mug about her."

"I believe you. Look at you—goes to show they can't take a good 'skin down." Ron and Swino exchanged hugs. For the first time, Ron showed off his new look to his best friend. He was a college boy now, complete with a small alligator on his red shirt and a pair of jeans that looked like they hurt, like they could squeeze orange juice from an orange. Ron was also sporting a flashy perm. Nice hair was a priority of his. In fact, he was obsessed with it.

"They did for a while there, though," Swino said. "So, you running circles around them white boys or what?" Swino was a true stereotypical Indian, always in a flannel shirt and old jeans, and this day was no different. And his nose! That damn thing pointed straight down even when he looked up. He was as rugged as they got.

"Ain't lost a race yet. So, what'cha wanna do?"

"Man, I need something to grease on."

"Come on. I know a place where they sell beer, too."

They went to a pizza shop, where Swino shoved a large pizza down his throat and Ron downed two pitchers of beer. Ron was more thirsty than hungry, but that's how it always was. Ron was a bonafide drinker. He could run like hell, he could even make it to school every day, but he could also drink like a fish. He had a love for it, a thirst that could never be quenched.

Once the two caught up on what gossip they had, they left. Business awaited. Actually, just more beer had to be drunk.

"Now what?" asked Ron with a smile.

"Booze and cruise?"

"Let's go, then. But we're picking up Thotes. I'm buzzing already, and you know how I get. And tonight the getting is going to get good."

"Right on. And I ain't seen that punk in . . ."

"Two years?"

"Fuck you."

"Don't feel bad. It's been two years for me, too."

"Don't you got to go to school tomorrow?"

"Nah, I told them I had personal agendas."

"Ooh, using them fancy words already?"

"Get in. We got some agendas to attend to our own selves," said Ron, and they got into his long brown LTD, which they called the Ark.

Even though Thotes was stocky and thick, he was still the ladies' man of the bunch. He had short feathered hair, and always dressed nice, even though he couldn't afford to. Thotes was sitting on his porch with four other nicely dressed Indian guys when he saw the Ark coming. He knew the car, so he met them at the curb.

"Holy shit!" shouted Thotes. "Who's this fuckin' ghost?" His silk shirt was unbuttoned farther down than it should've been, and his polyester pants looked as if they couldn't take any more ass.

"It's your daddy," said Swino. "Now, where's your momma at? Aye! You know they can't keep a good 'skin down."

"What are y'all all dressed up for?" Ron asked Thotes.

"Trying to get something going. Waiting on these broads to show up. They supposed to go AWOL from Rugged Indian Boarding School and buy up."

"No shit? Why don't you jump in with us," Ron asked. "We got two cases of brew in the trunk, and I need a driver. Feel up to it?" Thotes was the perfect guy for the job. Not only could he drive good when he drank, but he also knew where all the ladies would be later.

"I better," Thotes answered. "You can run, but you can't drive worth shit, boy. Let me tell these guys I'm splitting."

"Ha! Ha! Ha! Ha! Stayin' alive! Stayin' alive!" sang Ron as he and Swino watched Thotes walk. It made them laugh together.

In two shakes of a rattlesnake's tail, Thotes was driving the Ark, its trusty captain lounging in his own backseat. They drove out to the notorious back roads that circled NDN City. Anybody who was anybody did their drinking and driving out there.

A hundred potholes and two hours later—or ten o'clock to normal folk—they began to grow restless. At that hour, everyone got restless, and the back roads would become busy with Indians trying to find more Indians. And once that happened, parties would spring up in the damnedest places, in the middle of nowhere. They were ready to find one.

"Thotes, man, what about them AWOL girls you were talking about?" Swino asked. He was near drunk, blaming jail for making him a lightweight again, but he had always been a lightweight.

"I bet they're boozin' and cruisin' already. We'll see 'em."

"We better. I need to get laid my own self," Ron said. It was about that time.

"Don't forget, assholes, it's been two years since I've seen any action, so don't be trying to hog all the tail," pleaded Swino. The bad thing was, he was the most unlikely to get some. For some reason, chicks never really dug him.

"You can have my seconds," joked Ron, who had by then guzzled twelve beers.

"Bullshit, college boy. If he gets anybody's seconds, he'll get mine," said Thotes. It hit Ron deep inside, though, because he knew it was true. Even with his education and athletic ability, Thotes still got all the babes. Ron hated that.

"Yeah, whatever, man," Ron snapped. There was silence. It was so obvious that Thotes could kick his ass, but when Ron got drunk, he wasn't afraid of anybody.

"Where are the chicks at, Thotes?" Swino asked, to break the tension.

"I don't know. Maybe out at the Thomas Bridge," Thotes answered, brushing it off.

"Lezzgo go check that out. Fuck," Ron slurred. Swino turned up the eight-track, which played the Steve Miller Band's "Fly like an Eagle."

The Thomas Bridge was a bridge named after the famous drunkard Thomas M. Yeahpau. It was a small bridge—about four cars in length—located in the middle of nowhere. A small creek ran beneath it, and tall, dark trees bordered the banks. When they arrived, Thotes parked as close as he could to the bridge's cement railing.

All three boys got out and relieved themselves off the bridge. Waterfalls.

There wasn't a soul in sight, but with hopes of people showing up later, they stayed. Seconds turned into minutes, minutes into hours. They talked the kind of talk friends talk among themselves, and they laughed the way only friends can make each other laugh. It was loud and it echoed, until it was heard by the one thing that should not have heard it.

In the middle of a funny story, a certain stillness was broken, that comforting stillness that hid in the darkness and encompassed the boys. Then they heard it again—a noise in the trees, not too far from where they were sitting, near where they were parked. It wasn't a familiar sound. It was odd, indescribable. They stopped talking and the silence grew louder.

"Did y'all hear that?" whispered Swino.

"It came from over there," whispered Thotes, pointing up toward a tree.

"Probably Deer Lady," Ron joked.

"Yeah, like Deer Lady could climb a tree," said Swino.

"Maybe you could get some from her, Swino," Ron

said. That got all three of them laughing again, and there they were, back to their normal selves and loud as ever.

Then, all of a sudden, a large shadow emerged from the trees and headed straight toward them. The moon was bright and a shadow of such magnitude was hard to miss. It had wings! Without a second thought, they all ducked behind the Ark. Then a powerful wind blew over them. They huddled even closer together, none wanting to look, all three scared shitless. It was Ron who finally had the courage to glance up. And there it was. Spread across the night sky above them was an owl, a gigantic one, a grandmother owl. The worst kind.

"It's an owl!" yelled Ron.

The owl swooped down at them again. A strong wind blew over them, and this time there was also an ear-splitting screech. They were under attack!

It was do-or-die time. If they didn't get inside the Ark, they were sure to be owl food. Terrified, but still the bravest, Ron made a run for the backseat. He ran and he ran fast, faster than he had ever run. And in half of a half second, he was in the presumed safety of his backseat.

Before Ron could celebrate his escape, Swino and Thotes followed him in and dog-piled him. But they forgot one thing. They forgot to shut the door! Too late. They could hear the owl coming down again, so they all laid there, screaming like girls, as the owl made the most unusual sound. There was a loud clack, then more clack-ing. It got closer and closer and then something hit the open door. No one dared to look and see what it was. They knew.

"Get off me!" Ron yelled at his friends.

"Whatever you do, don't look at it!" yelled Swino.

There was another screech, louder than the one be-fore. The boys felt hot breath about their ankles. That was enough for Thotes. He pulled the necessary courage out of himself and climbed over to the driver's seat. Swino quickly followed, which left Ron alone in the backseat, with an owl trying to either eat him right there or drag him out of his car to eat him. Ron curled up into a ball. The Ark shook ferociously, making it difficult for Thotes to get the keys into the ignition. Then there was a mir-acle: the keys went in, the car started, and Thotes got the fuck out of there. Another screech was heard: the screech of tires. The Ark raced away at full speed.

"What was that, man? I mean, what just happened?" Thotes asked.

"Hell if I know, but that was crazy," Ron answered.

"This can't be happening. Owls don't attack people. My grandpa told me they're not supposed to," Swino said. His eyes were wide with fear.

"Fuck that. This one did. It almost pulled me out of the car. Did y'all see that shit?"

"Y'all know what?" Swino said. "Something bad is

going to happen to us. Take me home, Thotes." He was dead serious.

"Take you home?" asked Ron, who still wanted to drink. "Come on, man, that's just superstition."

"Superstition or not, I'm with Swino. Home don't sound bad at all. We're going back to town."

"But what about the chicks?"

"You can have 'em. We're taking our flat butts home while we still got 'em."

"Damn you guys. Okay, then, Swino, mind if I crash at your house tonight?" Ron asked. "I don't want to wake up my mom—you know how she gets." Ron's mom was a Christian and would be very disappointed, though not surprised, that he'd come all the way home just to drink.

"Come on, you know you ain't gotta ask. Just like old times already."

They continued down an old back road. Each downed a beer to calm his nerves. The drive was eerie. It was too quiet, and they were all too aware of the darkness surrounding them. They had taken the long way back to NDN City to avoid crossing the Thomas Bridge again.

It took miles and miles of worn asphalt, tall grass, and a good song on the radio to make them feel safe again. They had started laughing once more and Ron had started to tell them a story about something that had happened at college when they heard something else: three knocks, at the back window of the car, right behind Ron's head! Loud knocks, too, the kind that it was a test of strength not to answer. They all froze, they all swallowed their courage.

Knock! Knock! Knock!

"Don't turn around," whispered Swino, who knew the beliefs. His grandpa had taught him a lot before he died. Thotes and Ron didn't argue. Then, a louder knock. Thotes sped up.

KNOCK! KNOCK! KNOCK!

"Keep looking forward," Swino yelled. "Whatever you do, don't turn around!" He was fighting it; they were all fighting it. Something was drawing them to look. It wasn't curiosity. No. It was evil.

Ron kept repeating one word in his head: "science." He was an educated Indian now, and the science he had learned at college was getting the best of him. Things like this didn't happen, so what could possibly happen if he turned around and looked? Nothing science couldn't explain, nothing science couldn't fix. Indian superstitions were nothing more than elders' lies to children. His fear began to fade, and he almost felt embarrassed for being so afraid. There was a logical explanation for the knock at the back window; there had to be. So he turned, and he saw it! It was the owl—yellow eyes, blood-soaked beak, and all!

Ron screamed a scream only the dead could hear. He tried to turn away, but it was too late. It had him—with its eyes, its eyes, which soon became *her* eyes. Right then and there, the owl shape-shifted into something that would forever haunt Ron. Crouched on the trunk and looking into the back window was a horrible ugly old witch. She had the owl's yellow eyes and blood-soaked beak. Her hair was wild. Her face was so wrinkled, it didn't look real. She made a sound—a mix of screeching and laughter. It was horrifying. Meanwhile, as the car continued to speed down the road, Thotes and Swino were praying their asses off. But prayers rarely made it out of the back roads. Almost never.

The witch did what witches do best. She put a curse on Ron, a spell of some sort. His eyes were locked on hers, and his face began to move in ways it was not supposed to, impossible ways. His friends didn't look, but they could hear it, the sound of their longtime friend being disfigured. Then there came screams, ear-piercing screams that echoed through time.

Then silence, followed by the sound of Ron collapsing in the backseat. Then more screeching and laughter. But it faded, along with the sound of flapping wings, until they were no more. Thotes didn't dare stop; he drove even faster.

The lights of NDN City finally came into view. They'd made it! It was then that Swino turned around and looked at his friend. He couldn't believe what he saw. He turned to Thotes, not knowing what to say.

"What?" Thotes asked. "Is he okay?"

"No. No, he's not."

"Is he dead?"

"No. No, he's not."

Swino looked back at Ron again, though it was hard to bear. But they were the best of friends. Ron was unconscious, and his face was disfigured beyond recognition. Ron's mouth was over on the left side of his face, turned sideways, exposing his cheekbone. One eye was where his forehead should've been, and the other was on his chin. Both eyes were shut, big lumps on his face. And his nose — it was the worst, stretched all kinds of ugly ways. Swino had heard the old stories, the stories of owls twisting the faces of people who dared to disturb them. Now he was in one of those stories. He and his best friend, the best friend who had been on the path to great things. Swino started to sob.

Ron was still unconscious when they arrived in town. Swino and Thotes knew better than to take him to a white doctor or even to the Indian clinic doctor. They decided instead to take him to Grandpa Snake's cave in the Massacre Hills. Swino knew where it was, and who better to take Ron to than the strongest medicine man in the Indian Territory? He would know what to do.

A short time later they were inside the cave, standing in front of Grandpa Snake with their cursed friend. The cave was littered with bones, potions, gifts, and a single picture of Grandpa Snake and Grandma Spider in their early days, before the divorce. Grandpa Snake wasn't a typical medicine man. Actually, he wasn't even a man. He was a very large and very long snake, with a head about the size of an oil drum. A wise snake, respected more than feared. So wise he didn't even need to use words or motions to speak. He read minds. He had been expecting them.

Swino and Thotes left Ron there with the only person—or thing—that could save him. Then they returned to NDN City to confront a whole new terror— telling Ron's mother. As much as the news broke her heart, even she knew that Ron was now with the only person—or thing—that could save him. So she waited, along with everyone else.

Grandpa Snake had a rare gift. He could devour evil and then shed it along with his old skin. It took months and a lot of shedding, but Grandpa Snake eventually devoured all of the evil and every bit of the curse placed on Ron. Ron was able to return to his home in NDN City a new man, literally. His mind was never the same, never strong enough to go back to college. There was something different in the way he talked, in the way he walked, and in the way he remembered things and the way he forgot things. Everything changed. Everything except for his love of beer. That love became a habit, and that habit became an obsession, until Ron was consumed and it was all that was left of Ron's bright past.

PART III

X-Indian Women

Scarred are our women
tattooed with our pain

Scarred are their souls
filled with   holes
                inside of   holes

Scarred are their minds
forced to create a fatherless religion
praying their sons will once again love women
right

Scarred are their feet
carrying the weight of our people through
alleys of broken glass
never experiencing the soft plush
feeling of buffalo grass

Scarred are their hands
DNA spilling, loss of feeling
razor-sharp bills stealing

Scarred are their eyes
filled with visions
                    they wish not to keep
empty of tears
               no longer able to weep

Scarred are their mouths
dry and chapped   most men
from the wind of   are not worth the
loneliness   moisture

Scarred are their vaginas
men
trying to beat their way back inside,
never learning there's no running,
they can't
hide from
life

Scarred are their stomachs
speckled with beautiful signs of
life   proof
that our people will survive

Scarred are our women
tattooed with our race

Desire
1994–95

Mausape was gifted with a very powerful gift—the gift of story. With the right intentions, his gift could work miracles. With the wrong ones, his gift could bring about chaos, hate, and many other things associated with evil. And evil was always around the corner, waiting for him, hoping to influence the way he used his gift. Because of this constant presence of evil, Mausape was considered cursed. For any other reason, the Great Spirit would not have sent a personal guardian angel to protect Mausape throughout his life.

From the clouds above, the guardian angel kept a close eye on Mausape, shielding him from the influence of evil more times than he'd ever know. But she found the work of keeping Mausape safe worth the effort. He amused her.

When he was by himself, he wrote poetry. Nobody knew that except for her. She loved to read his poetry, too. It was an emotion on paper, in words, and that was very intriguing to any angel. What really intrigued this particular angel, however, was his appearance. She found him handsome and charming. He could make any girl smile. Why he spent time with the girls he did, she often wondered. As a matter of fact, she began to wonder too much. She began to lean farther and farther out from her cloud. Her curiosity with him soon gave in to desire. Then, she leaned out even farther from her cloud until she leaned so far out that she fell. She glided down toward earth, wings spread, unsure of what she had done. Could it be? She had hoped and prayed many times for just one chance to be close to Mausape, and maybe, just maybe, this was it.

A bolt of lightning struck one of her wings. The wing snapped off, and the angel went spinning down to earth like a helicopter out of control. All hope was denied, and she was sure to die. But, luckily, she had friends, and she called upon them. Actually, she screamed to them. Doves from all directions came to her rescue, catching her just in time, just above the trees. Then they laid her softly onto a blanket of snow, where she was born into flesh and blood—a full-grown woman, with wants and needs, with two wings and one curiosity: Mausape.

Mausape Onthaw, who was now seventeen, stepped

out of his dark blue Chevy Beretta onto the frozen ground. It was an ordinary Saturday night in NDN City for him, with the exception that he was riding alone, which was highly unusual. He normally never went out without Brando, Hoss, or Maddog. They were an entourage, not to mention business partners. And it was because of their business that they always traveled together, or at least in pairs, so that they could watch each other's backs. But that night, Mausape had some late-night errands to run and didn't get finished until midnightish. They all agreed to meet at Geronimo's at 1:00 a.m. It was now thirty minutes after, so Mausape assumed his friends / business partners were already inside. He walked into the large yellow barn, which was made of aluminum siding. Geronimo's was an all-night after-hours club that didn't sell alcohol but let patrons bring their own. Mausape carried in an open case of Brewer's beer.

It cost eight dollars to get in but was way worth it. Not only did the place have a good DJ, but it was the spot where all of the bomb-ass X-Indian beauties hung out. So many and all fine; it was like a bad-bitch buffet. Pretty good for eight dollars. As usual, his pressed clothes were all tucked in, and his freshly cut hair was styled to perfection. He looked all of the fine ladies up and down. They were everywhere. Then he scanned the terrain for his homeboys, but none were in sight. He made his way through a bunch of dancing bystanders. Still nobody. There was not a familiar face anywhere, so he found a nice spot along a wall close to the dance floor and waited.

Mausape was growing bored with his view of the speckled crowd when his eyes suddenly met hers. Actually, her eyes pierced his soul. Every sound vanished; every person disappeared. There was nothing, no one, except Mausape and the most beautiful X-Indian woman he had ever seen.

She was like a goddess. Her hair was as black as a soothing summer night in heaven, and it fell just a little down her back, the length Mausape was fond of. And her skin—it was the softest brown, an unbelievable brown, like a rich soil capable of producing abundant crops. Her lips, her eyes, and her nose—all perfect in every way. Then there was her body! It was a shrine made by the Great Spirit to remind men of his greatest creation. Where had she been all his life?

Mausape didn't know how long he had been staring at her when he once more became aware of noise, people, activity, but she caught him. Embarrassed, he tried to play it off by staring in another direction. Had he continued to look her way, he would have seen that she was smiling. He would have seen that she was approaching him, and it would not have startled him when she spoke.

"What do you say we dance?" she yelled over the music. The DJ had started a new song, a slow one.

"Yeah, okay!" he yelled back. She took his hand and led him to the dance floor. He couldn't help but wonder if the song playing was going to be "their" song. It sounded like Aaliyah.

She rested her arms comfortably on his shoulders, and they started a soft dance rhythm together. "Got a name?" she asked.

"Mausape. Mausape Onthaw," he answered, still in awe of the fact that he was this close to the girl of his dreams.

"Mausape. Does it mean anything?" she asked, though she already knew the answer.

"It means 'crazy' in my tribe's language."

"Are you?"

"Not really—it's just a name. What's yours?"

"Desire."

"Do you?" he asked, joking. It was a bad joke.

"Definitely," she replied, almost amused.

"No last name?"

"Not yet," she answered with a smile. Her smile was something Mausape could wake up to for the rest of his life. And her name—he could never grow tired of saying it. *Desire.*

"You from around here?" he asked.

"You could say that."

"Here alone?" he asked.

"Yeah."

"Cool."

"I know."

The two fell silent. Only smiles were left, but that was all they needed. His arms were right where they belonged, around her. Her arms were right where they belonged, around him. Fate felt wonderful.

It was love at first dance, but the slow song didn't last long enough. The DJ picked up the tempo with a hip-hop song that brought a crowd to the dance floor. Mausape and Desire separated, but only enough to move their bodies to the beat. Eye to eye, Mausape and Desire danced, touched, and moved to a pulsing rhythm.

After an hour of dancing to beats no Indian could drum, they grew tired and thirsty, so they went to find a table. Once they sat down, Mausape let it all out. He told her what he liked, what he disliked. He shared a few funny stories with her. His every word was like magic to Desire, and she was loving every spell he cast on her. Never had a conversation gone that well for him. But in the middle of one story, Mausape looked at his watch out of habit, and she took notice.

"Gotta go?" she asked with a hint of sarcasm.

"No, it's just that this place is about to close and—"

"I know. It sucks, don't it?"

"Yeah."

"But it ain't like we have to go our separate ways, right?" she asked with a certain look that pleased Mausape.

"True," he answered. It was exactly what he had

wanted to hear. It was also what she knew he had wanted to hear. She knew Mausape inside and out. Seducing him was nothing.

"I know we've just met, Mausape, but I have a really, really good vibe about you."

"You do? Well, I got a really good vibe about you, too."

"Why do you think that is?" she asked.

"I don't know. I guess it's chemistry. Some things go good together and some things go bad together."

"Which one are we?"

"Definitely good," answered Mausape, not the least bit embarrassed. It was a line, but he meant it.

"Take me home with you, Mausape," she blurted out. It caught him by surprise. It couldn't have been that good a line, could it?

"Now?" he asked, bewildered.

"Yeah," she answered, and smiled a smile that made Mausape think, *Damn!*

In no time, they were speeding toward NDN City and the duplex apartment in Bethlehem that Mausape shared with his longtime friend Brando. They found Brando passed out on the couch, sleeping the way a drunk guy sleeps—loudly.

Using his late-night manners, Mausape offered Desire a beer. She followed him into the kitchen, where they toasted a blissful night. After that, nothing more needed to be said. Their eyes said it all. They could both see love and nothing but love. It was meant to be.

"Mausape, what would you say if I told you that I want to please you in every way possible for as long as possible?" Desire asked seductively.

"I think I'd have to let you. But I got to be honest with you, Desire, there are some things about me, certain things I'm involved in, that might be hard for you to understand." Mausape was not proud of being a drug dealer. He was quite ashamed of it. But he had never opened up like that—never. With Desire he was honest. Maybe it was love.

"We all have our little secrets. I can accept yours if you can accept mine."

"But . . ."

"Shhh, just listen. I don't want to waste time on dating and all that getting-to-know-each-other stuff, Mausape. What do you say we just skip all of that so you and me can just be?"

"Just be?"

"Yeah, you and me," she answered; then she pulled Mausape to her and wrapped her arms around him.

"I like the sound of that," he said.

"Me, too," she whispered. Then they kissed.

As lovers do, they quickly found their way to the bedroom. Desire pushed Mausape down onto the bed. Mausape had a feeling that he might not get up for a very long time. She climbed on top of him, kissing him ever so generously. That's when it happened. Running his hands across her back, he felt something highly unexpected, highly unusual. There were lumps and other things— solid things—across her back. Whatever they were, they freaked him out. She sensed it and pulled away before he could take a look. She stood in front of him, innocent and uncertain.

"I think I should share my secret with you now," she said, "but I have to warn you, my secret will be the harder one to understand. I really don't know if you can handle what I'm about to tell you. Then again, you've seen these sorts of things before." Mausape could see hurt in Desire's eyes, and he didn't want to see it there ever again, ever.

"Seen what things?" he asked as gently as he could.

"Before I get into specifics, Mausape, I just want to say I love you." Her heart was breaking.

What had he done? How had he offended her? "I love you, too," he answered. Weird thing was, he meant it.

"Take a couple of deep breaths," she advised, and he did. Then she began: "I know everything there is to know about you, Mausape. I know about your grandpa and Deer Lady. I know about you and Brando and Maddog and Hoss and the whole operation you guys have—"

"Are you a cop?" he asked. Maybe what he had felt on her back was a wire. She was tapped!

His reaction hit her and her eyes watered. "No, I wish it were that simple. I know these things because . . ." she started.

"Because what?"

"Because I'm an angel. Your angel, Mausape." Tears ran down her face.

"What do you mean, you're an angel?" Mausape asked carefully.

"I know it's hard to believe, but I was sent by the Great Spirit to watch over you. And I have, Mausape, for far too long. Finally, curiosity got the best of me. Angels are not supposed to be so curious about such things."

"What things?"

"Mortality. Mortal love. Watching over you all these years, I grew to love you in a way I've never loved anything. My love is supposed to be equal for all things, but that is not the case with you. You've become special to me. I've grown to love you more than anything or anyone else. I had to see you close up; I had to smell you; I had to touch you; I had to feel you against me."

"What was that I felt on your back?" he asked, bringing her back to the subject of his interest.

"My wings. I still have them," she said, putting a hand up behind her.

"You can't have wings," Mausape said, disbelieving yet intrigued. "This is crazy."

"Yes, I can have wings, and I do."

"Like wings for flying?"

"Yeah. They were for flying, but I've broken them."

"I must be really drunk right now, or you just told me you're an angel with broken wings."

"You're not drunk."

"If your wings are broken and you can't fly, are you stuck here on earth?" He decided to go along with her story. It couldn't hurt.

"I wouldn't say that. I can't be stuck when this is the only place I want to be—with you, a mortal woman with a mortal love."

"Does that mean you're flesh and blood now? How did you . . . ?"

"I fell into mortality. That's how I broke my wings. It's a long story, but what's important is that I did it for you. I took a chance at mortality so that I could look at you through mortal eyes, touch you with mortal hands, and, maybe, love you the way mortals love. I have been wanting so much to experience the physical act of love."

"Sex?"

"Yes. The beginning of mortality and the end of immortality. It is said that when an angel lies with the son of man, her wings will fall from her body and she will have to remain on earth until the day she dies, as mortals do. This is what I have chosen to do for you, Mausape."

"I don't know what to say. I'm beside myself. An angel?" he asked, unsure, but sure at the same time.

"Just tell me you meant it," she said, "when you told me you loved me just now."

"I did. And I do."

A long silence followed. She was right about Mausape's having seen these sorts of things before, supernatural things. But questions remained. Was it bad? Would there be consequences? Or was it the best, most remarkable thing that had ever happened to him?

Now, Mausape *was* the type of guy to go with the flow and let things happen. Plus, he'd do just about anyone, so what was the big deal about Desire? She was the bomb and, with the body she was blessed with, so what if she had wings, or a tail, or anything else weird? She was Great Spirit–given, and Mausape knew he'd better hit that. He looked back into her eyes and, once again, felt that feeling he'd felt at the club—certainty that she was the one. He smiled, and it was exactly what she wanted to see. It hadn't all been for nothing.

"Can I see them?" he asked eagerly, like a little boy.

"Of course," she whispered. This was the moment. She began to pull her white dress down. Her breasts became visible. Amen. Then her dress dropped to the floor, leaving her in only a pair of white panties. Her skin was an infinite brown. Mausape watched patiently until, finally, they appeared. Slowly two wings unfolded from behind her back, full of the whitest feathers he'd ever seen.

Mausape was indeed fortunate. Standing before him,

exposed and innocent, was the most remarkable, the most beautiful woman he'd ever seen, with a pair of beautiful wings extending out from behind her. It was breathtaking.

"I'm the luckiest man alive," he said aloud. His mind was made up. He wasn't going to let her go, ever. "I love you," he told her, and he would never grow tired of telling her this.

Mausape took hold of her hips and pulled her to him. She smelled pure, like a miracle, what he wanted to smell forever. He kissed her stomach; she trembled. Her skin defined *soft*. He looked up into her eyes. He saw that she wasn't sure how it was supposed to happen. So, gently, he removed her white panties, pulling them down over her long legs. Mausape took time to enjoy the feel of her skin. He ran his hands up and down her body, behind it, between it. Her breath came harder. He stood and he kissed her, and he stroked her wings. They were soft, unrealistically soft. She gave way to touch next. Desire stroked his back, his mortal back. It was heaven on earth.

They lay down on his bed. Their bodies met. Skin against skin. Desire desired. Their hands explored every inch of each other. Mausape's fingers soon settled themselves where it was warmest. An unfamiliar feeling came over Desire and she didn't know how to react, how to sound, how to move. But that feeling overtook her, brought out the movements and sounds of a woman.

Soon it was all on him. It was his call. Since it was the last time she'd have wings, he figured he should enjoy them completely. They were so sexy. He stopped moving his hands and, getting no resistance at all, turned her onto her stomach. There was a sight to behold! Kodak never had shit on that moment. Up in the air, such perfect roundness, such perfect firmness, welcomed him. The muscles that held her wings to her back were something he would never forget. He savored the view: her wings, elegant, her body, flawless. Then he entered her.

At that sacred moment, when they were a single statue of love, their bodies locked into each other, her wings fell off. Actually, they shot off and hit the walls of his room. Surprisingly, there was no blood; the wounds in her back closed up immediately and healed over. It didn't seem to hurt to Desire at all. In fact, she turned and smiled at Mausape. As much as he wanted to say he was sorry, all he could do was fall beside her. He kissed her shoulder. Her sweat tasted as sweet as sugar.

Angels could never figure out the mortal fascination with sex. "Why?" was the big question in heaven. But now Desire knew why, and it was an answer worth knowing. Oh, it was worth knowing.

"There's no doubt about it," Mausape finally said. He was catching his breath. "You are an angel."

"*Was,* but thanks," Desire humbly replied. She was also trying to catch her breath.

"No. Thank *you,*" he said.

God knew what he was doing when he created Mausape. Desire caressed his face, but now it wore a funny look. "What's the matter?" she asked.

"I love you," he said, meaning it even more than before.

"I love you, too," she said back. Then they kissed.

"You weren't lying when you said they would fall off. They were outta here," Mausape joked.

Desire giggled. "I didn't know they'd shoot off like that."

"I'm just glad no one got hurt. I don't know how I would've explained that. So, there's no turning back now, huh?"

"Not for a lifetime."

"Good."

Still smiling, Desire closed her eyes and dreamed for the very first time. Mausape watched her. He was too excited to sleep. He had finally found love. He felt her skin again, and he whispered things to her that he had never said to anyone; he told her secrets. Mausape covered her with his favorite blanket to keep her from any chill. In her slumber, she smiled her thanks.

Quietly, he got up to get himself a drink of water. When he came back, he took notice of them—her wings. He picked them up from the dirty carpet and admired them for what he thought would be the last time. What was going to become of them now? She didn't seem to care too much for them anymore. Surely they couldn't be thrown away; they were too beautiful. Then the perfect idea came to him. He'd keep them, as a souvenir. With that thought, he placed them in a large gym bag and hid the bag deep inside his closet. The wings were his now: trophies of an undying love.

For the next week, Mausape and Desire didn't leave Mausape's bed for anything. Sex was strong in the air. It was the most Mausape had ever had, and Desire couldn't get enough of it. In between orgasms, they talked. Mausape mainly supplied answers to Desire's questions on mortality and on her duties as a woman.

But one day, a more serious topic arose: their future together. Mausape and his roommate, Brando, had agreed that neither could have a girlfriend living in the apartment with them. It was an invasion of privacy, a big no-no in what they did to make a living. Getting a new place to live was the only solution for Mausape and Desire. It wasn't a big deal to Mausape. He had the money. And as for the commitment, he was ready.

It was settled, and by the next week, he and Desire were looking for a new place. Brando didn't mind taking over the apartment expenses, but he was totally against his best friend moving in with a woman he had just met. It wasn't cool, and he told Mausape that he sensed something odd about Desire. She was too perfect. Mausape got a lot of good laughs out of that one. Within days, he and Desire had found a house to rent. It was just two miles outside of NDN City and it was where their life together would begin.

Mausape's relationship with Desire was almost too good to be true, which often made him worry and wonder if it was really as it seemed. Just out of curiosity, one day he asked his new wife what she did while he was out doing his business. She simply replied, "Wait for you." It was exactly what he wanted her to say. It was always like that, all the time. She said and did exactly what he wanted her to without his even having to tell her what that was.

Desire might have been the bomb in bed, but she worked miracles in the kitchen, too. How she had learned to cook so fast he didn't know, nor did he care. She could turn a slice of bologna into a steak. And her fry bread— oh, her fry bread! It was straight from heaven, and not even his grandma's could compare. In fact, it was so good that people always prayed before biting into it. They were either giving thanks or just praying for some more. There was nothing she couldn't fry up, and she knew all of his favorites: Indian corn, stew, luncheon-meat lasagna, and even grilled commodity-cheese sandwiches. And every night, like clockwork, dinner was ready by six. They seldom went out, and that was exactly how he liked it. He was raised on home-cooked meals and Desire didn't see any reason for that to change. Mausape lived like a king.

Months passed and everything seemed to be going perfectly—until one night, during one of their candlelit baths, when Mausape noticed two small lumps on Desire's back, right where her scars were, where her wings used to be. Reluctantly, she told Mausape the truth. They were new wings trying to grow. Tears filled Mausape's eyes, blurred his vision. Maybe it *was* too good to be true? Desire failed to give him a comforting explanation. She had no idea why they were growing back. An argument broke out. Maybe she was getting a second chance, she said, since the Great Spirit was a forgiving spirit. But she didn't want it, she said. Her place was with Mausape and she told him so, over and over. Regardless, he was hurt; he was threatened. They didn't talk for a long time, they didn't have sex for a long time, and day by day her wings grew. Ashamed of her past, she tried to hide them. Finally, he got up the courage to talk to her again. They were watching television; *Seinfeld* was on.

"When you were an angel, you were supposed to watch over me, right?" He was staring at her pretty face. It felt like an eternity since he had kissed her, tasted those lips.

"Yes, and I did. Any time something tried to harm you, I was there to protect you," she said, realizing how much she had missed his voice.

"But since you aren't in heaven anymore, who's watching over me now?" he asked. It was a good question.

"I don't know, but I'm sure another angel took my place."

"And if not?"

"I don't know," she answered. "I'm unsure. But I look at it like this—I'm still watching over you, from a lot closer now." She smiled again.

"But what if something were to happen to me and you couldn't protect me and I died? What would happen then?"

"What do you mean? Like, would you get into heaven? 'Cause if that's what you're worried about, I assure you, you have nothing to be afraid of."

"No, I'm talking about you. Where will *you* end up after you, you know, die? You've already left heaven. Think the Great Spirit will let you back in?"

"I don't know. That's a good question, too. I haven't really thought about it, but I'm sure I'd be able to go back."

"But how sure are you?"

"Not entirely sure," she admitted. She couldn't lie to him.

"So that means our future together is uncertain, right?"

"Isn't that part of being mortal? To be uncertain of what lies ahead? And why so many questions? Is something wrong, Mausape?"

"I was just thinking that maybe I'd like to spend eternity with you, that's all. Your wings, they scared me."

"How?" she asked with deep concern.

"What if the Great Spirit *is* giving you a second

chance? And if he is, don't you think you should take it? Because then you'd be in heaven and we could be sure we'd spend eternity together."

"But that means that, for now, I'd have to leave you," she said. Tears began to stream down her face.

"No, you wouldn't really be leaving me. You'd be able to watch over me again."

"Do you not want me here anymore? Did I do something wrong?"

"Of course not. I love you more than anyone I've ever loved. All I'm saying is . . . I don't know how to explain it to you. I'm just trying to be careful. I don't want to fuck this up, Desire. I'm not saying I want you to go; all I'm saying is that if there's a chance we can be sure we'd be together for eternity, we need to consider it." Mausape softly kissed her into comfort; then somehow, some way, they ended up making love. Sometimes words are better left unsaid.

The discussion was postponed, but Mausape still wanted to get his point across: he truly wanted to be with her forever. A week passed and her new wings were now full grown. They tried to make this pair fall off, too, but they remained. Desire hated them. Life went on, Desire catering to Mausape's every need, Mausape carefully planning his strategy.

Finally, he conceived a brilliant plot. Maybe. She always answered his questions with exactly what he wanted to hear. Maybe all he had to do was ask. Maybe all he had to do was command her to leave him and return to heaven. One night, to test this theory of his, he interrogated his wife, just as before, but with a different objective. He wanted to be sure that she would always say exactly what he wanted her to say. They were both in bed, and Mausape had to awaken her.

"Desire," Mausape whispered loudly. She opened her eyes and could see he wanted to talk.

"Yeah," she answered, yawning and wiping the matter from her eyes.

"If I ever cheated on you, what would you do?"

"Cheat on me? I know you wouldn't. I don't give you any reason to, do I?"

"No, but I'm saying, what if?"

"There would have to be plenty of reason for you to cheat on me," she answered, "so I'd try harder to please you where I had failed," she answered. It was exactly what Mausape wanted her to say.

"Do you love me?" he asked.

"What kind of question is that? You know I do," she answered. "I live for you and I'll do whatever I have to, to make you happy." That, too, was the answer he expected.

"So if that involved sucking my big toe, would you?" he joked, only half kidding.

The joke didn't get any laughter from her, though. Instead, she gave Mausape a look that told him she wanted only to make him happy. Seductively, she slid down to the foot of the bed and began to caress one of his big toes with her lips. It was surprisingly arousing. Before he knew it, she was showing all of his piggies a good time, one by one, two by two, playing his feet like a harmonica. He went with the flow, forgetting all about what he was trying to put to the test—something about something. It didn't matter. All that mattered right then was that his piggies got to where they were going, where Desire took them.

Her wings were a constant reminder that she was forsaking immortality for him. He loved her as a husband loves his wife, and Mausape believed that that kind of love was supposed to last forever, for eternity, far longer than their lifetimes. Fuck that "till death do us part" bullshit.

Desire was confirmation that there was a heaven, and Mausape wanted nothing more than to spend his eternity there with her. But Desire just couldn't comprehend that, and, pretending not to care, she sometimes walked around their house with her wings fully spread. It might not have been a big deal to either of them, but what if someone saw? What if someone found out? She would be taken away. That was an even more dreadful thought. Finally, one morning, before he left to handle some business, he confronted Desire.

"We need to talk," he said. They were standing near the front door.

"What's the matter?" she replied, aware that something was amiss.

"It's about your wings again."

"What about them?" she asked, but she knew.

"I've been doing some thinking, and I've concluded that you really should return to heaven."

Desire began to cry. "No" was all she could say. But it wasn't what he wanted her to say!

"But you do everything else I wish, so why won't you do this for me?"

"Because I want to stay here with you."

"Can you just try to look at this from my perspective? What we have here can end, but in heaven, it can be forever, for eternity. It'll never end."

"No, you don't understand. In heaven, I can't love you in the same way. I won't be able to. I'll be an angel and you'll be a soul," she said. She tried to stop crying, something Mausape had never seen her do before.

"You're giving me no other choice, Desire. I'm *commanding* you to leave here today and to return to heaven." It hurt like hell to say this, but it was for the best.

"Why do you not want me here anymore?" she cried.

"Please, just leave," he said, pointing at the door. He knew he couldn't make her understand, but hopefully she'd forgive him someday.

"No. Please, Mausape. I'll do anything."

"Do you want a divorce?" he threatened. "Is that

what it's going to take?" He knew the word "divorce" terrified her. It questioned her existence. She'd do anything to avoid it.

"No, no, no. I'll leave. Just don't . . . we don't have to do that. I'll leave."

"Okay. I'm going out to take care of some business, and when I return, I want you gone. Got that?" Mausape was in tears now, too. It was the hardest thing he'd ever had to do. He didn't know how, but he managed to walk out the front door and close it behind him. It was the last time he would see her for a long time.

"I love you. Oh, how I love you, Mausape," he could hear her say, between sobs.

"I love you, too," Mausape said to himself. He could barely see as he drove away from all he'd ever wanted. But he heard her sobs forever.

Desire could not understand why he had made his decision, nor could she make him understand why she defied it. Their love had to be that of mortals, no matter what Mausape thought he knew.

Her solution was simple. She would leave, but she wouldn't return to heaven. Because she had seen, many times, that time brings people back together. Time brings regret, and regret can bring forgiveness. She would leave, only to return when forgiveness was close at hand. And so she packed. But her wings, her damn wings! She hated them and knew they would make things difficult for her in the outside world. In an enraged frenzy, she pulled hard at one. Something happened. Her wing began to separate itself from her body. The pain was excruciating, but she pulled again, harder, and after a few more tugs, it came off completely. Blood splattered her white feathers and onto the floor. The next one came off more quickly but just as painfully. Before she knew it, she was wingless again. With bandages over her wounds, she left and set out to find what the world had to offer a wingless angel, at least until forgiveness found Mausape's troubled heart. Desire had been mortal for some time now, but it wasn't until she had done what *she* wanted that she became a woman.

Mausape returned home the next day, suffering from a hangover. He had drowned his sorrows in the company of his friends Maddog, Hoss, and Brando, who were glad that he was back in the game. Normally, Mausape would've been happy to be back home. That wasn't the case now. Far from it. Desire was not there to greet him, to welcome him with a smile. He cried like a baby, heartbroken and hoping that Desire could see. He wept in their bedroom and on their favorite couch. He thought he was going to weep for weeks. During his darkest hour, something caught his attention. Blood. Leading to the trash. Blood. And, to his disbelief, there was a great surprise waiting for him there. Desire's wings! What the hell were they doing in his trash? What did it mean? One thing was for sure: she was out there, somewhere in the world, far from his protection.

Mausape hid the wings with the others, in a large gym bag in his closet. And there they stayed while Mausape patiently awaited her return. And thus, somewhere, deep in the Indian Territory, there is a man with all the hope in the world, and a collection of angel wings in his closet.

A Dozen Roses
1996

THURSDAY NIGHT

"I can't believe you fucked her! I thought we had something, Hoss!" yelled Every-Rose-Has-Its-Thorns. Everyone simply called her Rose, though. Her creamy skin was now red with rage. Even when she was angry, she was still attractive as hell. Her permed hair was tinted and fixed to look elegant, and her makeup was applied with utmost perfection. Every X-Indian woman in NDN City envied her, some because of her beauty, some because of her sophistication. At eighteen, she was also very mature. At least most of the time she was. Hoss was known to bring out the worst in her.

"Something like what?" snapped Hoss. "The only time you come over is when you're drunk." Hoss was

Rose's opposite—rugged and a little rough around the edges. He was also eighteen.

"What's that supposed to mean? You know what?" she said. "Fuck this. I'm outta here." She stormed out, slamming the door behind her.

"Damn women," muttered Hoss, taking a seat on his couch, inside his home, in the run-down neighborhood of Jerusalem, located on the outskirts of NDN City. Rose's anger and jealousy kind of shocked him. He had suspected that she had feelings for him, but she had never confirmed those suspicions. Actually, he believed that she had just been using him for late-night sex on them nights when she got drunk and horny. Not to say that he didn't love them nights or the thought of being used by Rose. To tell the truth, it was the bomb. He couldn't get enough of her beauty, which, from head to toe, was close to six feet of the sexiest terrain he'd ever charted.

On top of being sophisticated and beautiful, Rose was highly intelligent. She had graduated at the top of her class at NDN City High and was currently attending a local college, with hopes of transferring to the University of the White Man's Ways in the W.M.T. soon. Hoss, on the other hand, didn't even graduate high school, and the only education he had was the one gotten on the streets.

Police sirens screamed outside of Hoss's house, reminding him that not too many women from Babylon, the classy neighborhood, would drive anywhere near

Jerusalem. It made him realize just how much Rose must really care for him. Hell, people who lived in the Jerusalem neighborhood rarely drove through it. He was about to lose the best thing that had ever kept him company at night. There was no denying that Rose was the best he'd ever do, because beautiful, sophisticated, and intelligent women were a rare treasure in NDN City.

He lay down to think his situation over. Hoss knew that Rose didn't like the idea of him being a player, a ladies' man. But it was something he had no control over; he loved the ladies and the ladies loved him back. Not only that, but he was obsessed with sex, an addict, a sexaholic who always loved a little variety. Not even Rose, being the hellified fuck that she was, could stop him from fucking other women. And that was the problem. She had just found out about him fucking someone else. It was just a one-night stand, but a betrayal nonetheless. He didn't know why he did it; he just had to. His unfaithful ways weighed heavy on him, like a curse—the curse of the player.

Hoss thought long and hard on love and what it was. Love was only a word to him; he never took it seriously. But if he had ever loved anyone, it was Rose. Sooner or later, the time would come when he would have to settle down with one woman, and she was the perfect candidate. So he had to make up with her, which was going to be some task. He tried out idea after idea. Finally, he thought of the perfect making-up gift. It was so obvious.

He would buy her roses! It was the perfect gesture, seeing how her name was Every-Rose-Has-Its-Thorns. Duh! But the brilliance of his plan was to not only get her roses, but to take them to her town house and leave them at her doorstep, along with a sweet apology letter. When she awoke the next morning and left for work, she would find them and see how sincerely he wanted to be with her. He had his moments.

Hoss made a late-night trip to the grocery store, where he found the perfect arrangement of roses in a red heart-shaped vase. He purchased his $24.99 destiny and drove to Rose's town house in Babylon, where he knew she was fast asleep. With the stealth of a ninja, he placed the arrangement at her front door, along with a note that read, *A dozen roses for the only rose in my life, the rose that someday I will call my wife. Please forgive me—I'm only a stupid man.—Hossy*

He had called his friend Mausape earlier that night for help with writing the note. Hoss was that desperate, and he knew Mausape was gifted with words. As soon as everything was placed perfectly at her doorstep, Hoss left as quietly as he had come.

The sound of banging on his door awoke him. He looked at the time. It was 7:45 a.m. Right away, he guessed who it was, but he acted surprised to see Rose standing on his porch, holding the roses.

"Hi. Sorry to wake you," Rose apologized. She looked confused.

"No, I'm glad you came by," Hoss replied, which brought a big smile to her face. "Wanna come in?" he asked.

"Yeah," she said, walking back in through the door she had slammed shut the night before. "I just want to thank you for your gift. It really means a lot to me."

"I was hoping you'd like it."

"I got you a gift for you, too."

Rose set the roses down on Hoss's kitchen table. Hoss closed the door behind him, and before he could utter another syllable, her tongue was in his mouth. And after a long kiss, he found himself on the couch, Rose tearing at his body with her lips, her tongue, and those fingers of hers. It was safe to say that Rose had forgiven him, but she proved it even more when she stood and undressed. Sometimes it was a good day to die; sometimes it was a good day to fuck.

Hoss pulled her slender body closer so he could breathe in the unique scent of her nakedness. Then he helped her onto his lap and she rode him like she was riding a warhorse into battle. She was his war princess, and soon war cries filled the air. Native love. Sex in love was the bomb. He would have to buy her roses more often!

When she had regained her composure, she got up and casually got dressed, leaving Hoss on the couch, nude.

"You just going to lay there like that?" she asked, joking.

"Just until you get back."

"You'll be there until Sunday, then. I'm going to see my grandma in Comancheville for the weekend. That's why I came by so early. I wanted to give you something to hold you off until I get back."

"So it's like that? Wham, bam, thank you, man. I see how you are."

"If you promise to behave while I'm gone, I might give you a little something extra when I get back."

"You better," he joked.

"You and your friend be good. Momma will be back in a few days. I gotta go now," she said. She leaned over and kissed Hoss, then stepped out of his home, closing the door quietly behind her.

Damn, it feels good to be a player, Hoss thought to himself.

FRIDAY NIGHT

"What up, dog?" Hoss asked, holding the phone to his ear and stirring a pot of ramen noodles on the stove.

"We still on for tonight?" Maddog asked.

Hoss had almost forgotten about their planned trip to the infamous after-hours club Geronimo's. "Hell, yeah."

"I thought you were going to puss out on me, man."

"Fuck that." Since Rose was out of town, there was

no reason to change their plans. "I'll pick you up around ten. Deal?"

"Deal. I'm ready to get my club on. Got my snagging briefs on, too. Gah!"

Hoss got ready in a hurry. On his way out, he noticed the arrangement of roses still on his kitchen table, so for safekeeping, he took them to his bedroom.

Hoss picked up Maddog in Silver, his gray '84 Cutlass. It was already eleven o'clock. First things first. They picked up a runner and got their beer. Two cases of Brewer's beer was enough to do the job, but barely. They drank like it was going out of style. After dropping off their runner, they headed to the club, which was located in the Massacre Hills, just outside NDN City. What was so good about this particular club was that they never IDed anyone, ever. But Geronimo's didn't open until midnight, so Hoss and Maddog cruised the back roads, reminiscing about the good ole days, until it was time.

They ended up not pulling into Geronimo's parking lot until two in the morning. Carrying half a case each, they made their way in. It was packed, and right off the bat, Maddog found a long-haired X-Indian chick that he knew sitting at a small table with a friend. They invited the two and their beer to sit with them, too. Maddog didn't waste any time claiming his snag for the night. Within minutes, he had his arm around the girl he knew, the thicker one of the two. He liked them thick, what he called Heinz 57 babes. Hoss was already checking out the friend. Her name was Desire. Her body was blessed, and covered in a tight white dress that Hoss wanted to see gone.

Hoss and Maddog had already known who she was. She was Mausape's wife, or ex-wife; they had separated some months ago. She was even finer than Hoss had remembered. No wonder Mausape had kept her hidden away.

While Maddog busied himself with his snag's lips, Hoss preoccupied himself with the woman who had broken his friend's heart. They shared conversation and a few innocent dances. The more time he spent with her, the more she blew his mind, in a way most girls could only ever dream of doing.

Many beers later, Hoss found himself drunker than he wanted to be. He ran his fingers carelessly through Desire's silky hair while she talked on and on about love and forgiveness. It was looking good for him, though. She had made a few passes at him throughout the night, and he had done the same. It was just a matter of time.

When the club closed for the night, Hoss had one intention only, to take Desire home and have wild sex with her, no matter what the consequences might be. Luckily for him, Maddog had already decided to go home with his snag. Hoss made his move and somehow talked Desire into going home with him—but just to talk some more, of course.

It was a long drive back to Hoss's home in Jerusalem. Once there, they went through the usual boring conversations people have when they are drunk, alone together, and know they are about to have sex. Finally, a pause gave their lips time enough to find each other, and they made their way to the bedroom. Hoss went into his usual foreplay routine. He kissed her breasts—

"Are them roses?" Desire asked, looking at the arrangement of flowers on his dresser.

"Yeah," he answered, uninterested.

"I want one," she said. Hoss stopped, sat up, and grabbed two roses from the vase.

"Close your eyes," he commanded, but his voice was sweet. Desire closed her eyes.

Hoss slid a rose across Desire's beautiful face and over her neck. Her moans were as soft as the petals touching her skin. He slid the other rose along her brown legs, giving her goose bumps. After the intense arousal with the rose had gone on long enough to make even him wet, he drew a rose along her inner thigh and all the way up, under her short dress. She spread her legs, welcoming it. He had hit the spot, struck the mother lode. Her legs twitched and tightened. She enjoyed it immensely, so much that she slipped off her thong. Hoss slid a rose across her bush. She jerked and moaned. Damn, it was sexy!

Hoss was tempted to drop the roses and get right to the point, but the floral foreplay intrigued him. He had to buy roses more often! Hoss carefully unzipped her dress. That's when he saw the two large scars right over her shoulder blades. He had found a flaw in her perfect appearance, but it was nothing, really. She was just one perfect curve after another. Hoss drank in her glory.

It had been a while since Desire had had sex, but it was all coming back to her, fast. Somehow, in some way, she took control. She helped Hoss out of his clothes, and, just like that, they made wild, sweaty, early-in-the-morning love. And when it was all over, just like that, they passed out, holding each other as drunk lovers do.

Hoss awoke in the afternoon to find Desire gone. In her place, there was a rose and a note that read *Please don't tell Mausape about this.*—*Desire*

Damn, it feels good to be a player, Hoss thought to himself.

SATURDAY NIGHT

Hoss, Maddog, and their new friend Tyronimo were all chillin' at Hoss's. It was an innocent night. They were just drinking beer and watching a boxing match when there came an unexpected knock at the door. To Hoss's surprise, it was Morning-Dew, a rumored sex goddess whom he had known for some time. They hadn't actually fucked yet, but they were both willing to change that. Morning-Dew had actually been one of Brando's girls, but now that he had settled down with Morning-Dew's cousin, Two-Rivers-Flowing-Together, she was available.

In a quick flashback, Hoss recalled a conversation with her earlier that week. In that conversation, he'd invited her to his house to watch the fight with him but said that he would be alone. Damn.

"Can I come in?" Morning-Dew asked. She was a serious brown, a rugged beauty with long straight hair. Her juicy ass was squeezed into a pair of tight jeans, her well-proportioned breasts into a tightly laced shirt. Her curves were to die for.

"Where's my manners? Come on in. You want something to drink?"

She strutted over to his couch, her ass rocking back and forth, hypnotizing him. Brando could pick 'em. He had once told Hoss, "If you ain't had Morning-Dew, you ain't had shit."

"Got anything besides beer—something stiff?" she asked slyly.

"Got some Captain Morgan. How about a Captain Mo' and Coke?"

"Sounds good for now." Then, to his friends: "So who's winning?"

"Tyson's fucking him up. I give him another round."

Maddog looked like he hadn't stopped drinking from the night before. Probably hadn't.

"Am I late?" Morning-Dew asked Hoss.

"Nah, not really. I didn't think you'd show up."

"My word is my bond. I thought you knew that, Hoss."

"I do now. Here you go," he said, and handed Morning-Dew her drink. Hoss took a seat and got comfortable. The referee in the boxing match started the count, making it all the way to ten. Maddog and Tyronimo got up and celebrated.

"Let's go get that fuckin' money, Ty," said Maddog. "Hoss, man, we're outtie."

"Thanks for the beer, Hoss," said Tyronimo, who winked at Hoss on his way out. Just like that, Ty and Maddog were gone. Hoss wished he could've walked out with them, but he knew, and they knew, that a player does not turn down sex, especially with someone like Morning-Dew.

"Alone," she said, staring at Hoss. "Just how I like it."

"Yeah." Hoss knew she was there for only one thing, but he needed a little more motivation. He made more drinks.

A dozen or so mixed drinks later, they were both drunk enough to make it okay for them to have sex on their first date. They grabbed each other and started to tongue wrestle. Hoss slid on top of her. Then he lifted her shirt and began a series of kisses leading to her breasts. He wanted to see their enormous beauty. There was nothing like X-Indian women's breasts. Hoss was so turned on by her that he prematurely pulled down his pants, revealing just how turned on he was. Morning-Dew was impressed.

"Hold up, killer," she said. It was unclear if she was talking to him or his erection. "Let's go to your room."

"All right," he said.

"Why don't you put some music on?" she said, giggling, and then disappeared into his room.

"Cool, just give me a minute."

Hoss found his Jodeci CD and started it on the song "Freek 'N You" to set a freaky-deaky mood. He went to the bathroom and did a quick check on himself, making sure he had cleaned off Desire's juices well enough to get an oral treat. Then he practically ran to the bedroom, where he was greeted by the sexiest sight he'd ever seen.

Morning-Dew was lying on the bed on her back, completely naked. She was shaved. But what compelled him the most was the way her long black hair blended in perfectly with his black satin sheets. It looked as if she was lying on a bed of her own hair. Then he noticed something else. There were rose petals all over his bed. Rose's rose petals!

"So, what do you think?" Morning-Dew asked. "Ever fuck in a bed of roses?"

"Damn" was all Hoss could whisper.

Their bodies came together violently, explosively. Rose petals went flying everywhere. Hoss smeared them over her breasts all the while he was behind her.

When they were done, their sweaty bodies were plastered all over with rose petals. The lust and alcohol had drained them. They both quickly fell asleep and dreamed of flowers.

The next morning, Hoss awoke to the scent of roses. He and Morning-Dew were both rose scented. He savored the sweet fragrance. The bed-of-roses idea was something he would definitely have to use again. And he did, as soon as Morning-Dew woke up. They made floral love once more. The floral aroma grew even heavier. Finally, Hoss and Morning-Dew exchanged lies, saying they'd call each other, and she left, leaving Hoss smelling better than he had ever smelled.

Damn, it feels good to be a player, Hoss thought to himself.

SUNDAY NIGHT

Hoss was sitting alone in his living room watching *The Simpsons* when there was a knock at the door. It was the visitor he'd been expecting: Rose. She had a smile waiting for him, so he smiled back.

"About time," he joked.

"Ah, did you miss me?" she asked in a baby voice.

"Immensely. How was your grandma?"

"Good. So, what did you do all weekend?"

"Nothin' really."

"Yeah, right. By the way, did I leave my roses here?"

"Sure did. See how you are?" he joked. "I get you something special and you just leave them lying around anywhere."

"I'm sorry, Hossy. Really, I am. Where are they?"

"Back here," he answered, and he led her to his bedroom, where a single rose stood in the heart-shaped vase. She gave Hoss a suspicious look.

"What happened to the rest of them?" she asked.

"They're right here," Hoss said, carefully turning down the covers on his bed. The bedsheets were covered in rose petals. Rose was speechless.

Together, they climbed into the bed of roses.

From underneath one of his pillows, Hoss pulled out a single rose and, in bull-fighter fashion, put it between his teeth. That made Rose laugh. He loved to hear Rose laugh. Hoss surprised her when he went over her body with that one rose, slowly, inch by inch. Rose loved it. Her creamy color gave way to crimson. Her heavy breathing gave way to panting. And soon the rose gave way to his tongue. Before they knew it, they were making love. Petals were everywhere again. It was the most beautiful moment Rose had ever had with Hoss. She had never seen this side of him, and she instantly fell in love with it. In a bed of roses, they made love for the second time as a couple *in* love.

"You should buy roses more often," Rose said after it was over.

"Seriously?"

"If you don't, I will."

"I thought you'd might like it," he said. There was silence, then—

"You know what I think?" she said.

"What's that?" he asked.

"I think our relationship is blooming into something really special."

They smiled at each other. "Yeah," he answered. Hoss never wanted to look into another woman's eyes. At least for the time being.

Damn, it feels good to be a player, Hoss thought to himself.

PART IV

How It Feels to Be an X-Indian Man

The only thing I was taught was how to
Survive.
Being imprisoned in this land, I am not
Free.
Every day I wake up is a good day to
Die.

Everything is all right, or so you
Think.
I got generations of generations of building
Hate.
And all I can do about it is
Escape.

And I don't cry. X-Indian men don't cry; we only escape.
I escape as much as I can, until my X-Indian woman asks me,
"When are you going to make war with the white men and get
our land back?"
I tell her, "After this beer, after I come down, after *The Simpsons,*
after another forty hours of work, after I die
and go to the heaven the white men have taken from us also."
Then I cry,

And realize I am neither man nor X-Indian.

You Win!
1999

"Can I turn it, Momma, can I?" asked Li'l Hoss. His favorite wrestling show, *WCW Monday Night Nitro,* was about to start. Only four years old, and already he had acquired his dad's insatiable appetite for violence. His mother was young, like most mothers in NDN City, so she didn't really understand the effect all that violence had on her budding offspring.

"Go ahead," she said, "but turn it down." Every-Rose-Has-Its-Thorns had gained a little weight after having Li'l Hoss, but it was in all the right places. Even in a pair of old jeans and a faded T-shirt, she still turned heads.

"You know that's all fake," said Storm, from a couch in the living room. "I mean, who keeps bouncing off ropes like that?" Storm was Rose's cousin. Many thought she was just as beautiful as Rose, but in a different way. Storm's beauty was a tattered beauty, touched way too often. Unspecial.

"Shhh, don't tell him that," Rose whispered. "He likes it."

"I don't see why men like this. Hell, women should be the ones watching it. Look, it's just a bunch of fine-ass men in their underwear beating each other up. Damn, he could beat me up any day."

"It's more like a soap opera, Storm, but for guys."

"It is, isn't it? Never thought of it like that. Speaking of guys, where's Hoss?"

"Uh, don't get me started."

"What'd he do this time?" Storm asked, but now she was really paying more attention to the wrestling.

"He's avoiding me right now. And for good reason."

"What happened?"

Rose motioned for Storm to follow her into the kitchen, out of earshot of Li'l Hoss. Storm was wearing a pair of thin cotton shorts, the ones that Rose had asked her not to wear around the house. Rose had caught her boy staring at Storm's assets a few too many times. And it wasn't her boy Li'l Hoss, either, but her husband.

"He knows I found out about him and that girl from Apacheapolis," Rose told Storm.

"What girl in Apacheapolis?"

"That one I told you about. Remember? I told you

about how he's been going to Apacheapolis a lot lately. Someone told me that he's fucking some hoe there named Shadow. That's what I've been meaning to ask you. Do you know a Shadow from there?"

"Shadow, Shadow, Shadow. Nope, doesn't ring a bell. But I ain't been out that way in a mad minute, not since I started staying here with you."

"Anyways, this morning, when he came in, I asked him where he'd been all night, and he just said, 'Cruisin'.' So I said, 'Where? Apacheapolis?'"

"But you don't know for sure that he's been cheating, do you?"

"Kind of."

"How? Did he tell you something?"

"No. No, nothing like that. This morning, I guess he was pretty drunk, because when he came home, he passed out as soon as he hit the bed. And I couldn't sleep. I was just lying there, thinking, you know, wondering if he was really cheating on me. I mean, I'm twenty-two now. I'm too old to be playin' games. Plus, we have a son together. Anyways, while he was asleep, I pulled his boxers down and smelled his . . . you know."

"What? His dick?"

"Yeah."

Storm laughed. "Girl, you ain't any better than them guys! They supposed to be the dogs, and here you are, sniffin' around down there. Ha, ha, ha!" Storm usually respected, even envied, Rose, but at this moment, Rose deserved to get clowned on.

"You going to listen or what?" Rose asked. She wasn't trying to be funny.

"Yeah, just wait up. I'm sorry. Go ahead."

"Well, I smelled it, and guess what?"

"Do I have to?" Storm asked, trying not to smile.

"Ah, forget it, then."

"Okay, okay. What?"

"I smelled poo-nanny."

Storm laughed, even harder than before. She hadn't heard anything that hilarious in a long time. "You smelled what?"

"Vagina. *Payh*. Okay, I smelled pussy. There."

Storm kept on laughing, until tears smeared her makeup. "Damn, girl. I knew you was crazy, but this is too much. You're making my sides hurt."

"What the hell's so funny about that?"

Storm finally stopped laughing. Rose was dead serious. "Nothing. Nah. It's just, I can't believe you called it poo-nanny. I'm sorry."

"If you're done, let me continue. That pussy smell didn't come from me, so I bet he was in Apacheapolis with that hoe last night."

"That is hard evidence, no pun intended. But I don't know what to tell you, except confront him about it."

"That's what I was going to do, but I ended up falling

asleep, and when I woke up, he was already gone. He knows his ass is in for it."

"I don't think you need him, anyways. I know you two have been together for a while, but just think about it—he's never around, he never helps you out with Li'l Hoss, and he's always drinking up all y'alls' money, like he's the one working."

"It's not his fault he can't get a job. It's those damn drug charges."

"That's another thing. He's been in and out of jail a lot lately. You just need to get a new man. I know you can do a lot better than him, Rose, for reals."

"Maybe, but it's easier said than done. I think I've just been living on hope for way too long. I always thought he might change his ways. Well, he did quit selling, and I'm proud of him for that. Maybe it's me."

"Don't even go there. He's a dog, Rose."

"Yeah, you're right. I'm sure this isn't his first time, and he'll probably do it again. Maybe I should just get rid of his ass."

"I'm telling you, girl. There are plenty of fish in the sea."

Li'l Hoss was enthralled by *WCW Monday Night Nitro*. The first match was over, and the show was interrupted for a commercial break. The first commercial was one he had been seeing a lot lately—a Brewer's beer commercial.

It opened with a scene of four guys drinking Brewer's beer while watching a football game on television.

"Brewer's beer," voiced-over an announcer. "It's great for any occasion! And now even better!"

"This sure is a good game," said Guy 1.

"Yeah! Go! Go! Go!" yelled Guy 2.

"Hey, hand me a beer!" shouted Guy 3 to Guy 4.

"Here you go, buddy," replied Guy 4, handing Guy 3 a beer. Guy 3 opened his beer, and a voice from inside the can shouted, "You win!"

"No way!" exclaimed all four guys at the same time.

"Yes, it's that simple. Just open a can of Brewer's beer—great for any occasion—and you can become a millionaire! It's true. The lucky person who finds the winning can will win one million dollars! So go out there and get some Brewer's beer—great for any occasion—and you could end up *one million dollars* richer!" The announcer, who was now visible, stood next to a neatly stacked bundle of money and a pyramid of Brewer's beer cases. He was a creepy-looking white man.

There were two X-Indian guys, both bald as hell, sitting on the bank of a lake, fishing and drinking beer. One of them looks to the other one and says, "I caught Rose smelling my dick last night."

"What the fuck?" Maddog asked, almost choking on his beer.

"I think she knows about me and Storm."

"What's that got to do with her smelling your *thookaloo*?"

"That's how chicks do it. They can smell another girl's scent."

"Really? But you didn't fuck anybody last night. Or did you?"

"Actually, I did. After I dropped you off last night, I drove home but parked at the end of my street. I walked to the house and up to Storm's bedroom window. She let me in. Next thing I know, we're both buck naked and goin' at it like crazy. She was moaning all loud and shit, too. I think Rose might have heard us."

"Are you for reals, Hoss? You fucked Storm in your own house, with Rose in the next room?"

"I know, but I just couldn't help myself. Storm's got some good-ass *payh*. You know a Native can't turn down good *payh;* that's why we had a lot of wives back in the old days. Anyways, after I finished, I went back to my car and drove up like I was just gettin' home. Then I acted like I was all faded so Rose would let me pass the fuck out. I guess she thought I went straight to sleep, because I heard her crawling around and shit. Then she fuckin' pulled my boxers down! That's when I opened my eyes a little and saw her sniffing around my dick."

"I don't know. If Rose knew you were fuckin' Storm, shit would've went down right then and there.

Storm would be dead and your ass would be in the hospital. You know how crazy Rose gets."

"That's why as soon as she fell asleep, I boned the fuck out. For all I know, Storm might be dead. Storm. I just wish that things hadn't gotten all complicated for us, her getting kicked out of her mom's house. It was easier then, with her in Apacheapolis. I'd go see her and she'd always want to get high and then she'd wanna fuck. I miss that. On the reals, dog. In the three hours her mom played bingo, me and her would do some freaky-deaky shit, shit you wouldn't believe. And now she's right there, right in front of me all of the time. It's torture—I'm telling you."

"Was last night the first time in a long time?"

"No, I still hit it. Sometimes I pick her up somewhere and we drive out to one of my spots and we go at it."

"What spots? The only one you got is the ole abandoned oil well. You need to stay away from there, for reals."

"Fuck that, it's the best place to go. Think I'm scared of some fuckin' ghosts?"

"Fuck the ghosts, I don't want any pigs sniffin' around there. Why don't you just get a motel room?"

"I would, but you know how it is. Too many people like to talk around here."

"Either way, Hoss, you're pissing in the wind."

"Maybe. But I just need to find a job, so I can save some money up to get my own place. Build my shit back up, like when Brando was around. Then I could break up with Rose, and Storm could move in with me."

"So Rose don't do it for you anymore?"

"Nah, not anymore. All she does now is bitch, bitch bitch bitch bitch bitch. And I've had it with that shit. I love Li'l Hoss and all that, but I gotta get away from Rose, and fast. I swear, her bitchin' is about to turn me into a fuckin' woman beater."

"You know, I thought I would never see the day you two split up," Maddog said. "I know you get yours here and there, but you always go back to her." Maddog pulled a joint out of his shirt pocket and lit it.

"Things change, dog," said Hoss. "Things change." He opened another beer.

"Do you think Storm *would* move in with you? She's the bomb, man, and ain't she hooked up with Tyronimo?" Maddog took a hit off the joint.

"Fuck Tyronimo, half-breed muthafucker. I make sure I knock her to sleep every time, boy," Hoss bragged. He grabbed the joint and took a hit himself.

"Ah, I hear that, man. You be like, wham, bam, see you in the morning, ma'am. I'll be doin' hoes the same way."

"Damn, dog, I'm gettin' fucked up," Hoss said, and exhaled a large cloud of brain cells.

It was getting late. Rose had just returned from her mother's house, in Babylon, where she had dropped off

Li'l Hoss for the night. Rose did not want him around when his dad returned. It wasn't going to be pretty.

Sitting on a secondhand couch, staring at the television, she waited. The TV wasn't even on. She was heavy in thought, her anger building every time she imagined Hoss with another girl. Yeah, another girl, not a woman. A woman wouldn't have done such a thing. This was it. This was the last time, the last straw. Her cousin was right. Something drastic had to be done. Hoss had to go. And as soon as he walked through that door, she was going to let him know.

In a room adjacent to the living room, Storm lay sleepless. She was thinking, too, mainly about how she could end her torrid affair with Hoss. He wasn't worth it. Why she had gotten herself mixed up with him in the first place, she hadn't a clue. Maybe because it was a little dangerous; maybe because she was bored. Whatever the reason, Rose was on to them. She knew about the trips to Apacheapolis; she was even close to getting the name right. "Shadow" wasn't too many syllables away from "Storm." Shit was going to go down if Storm didn't put a stop to it soon. Hoss had to go. And as soon as she got the chance, she was going to let him know.

Hoss and Maddog went fishing frequently, never catching anything but a good buzz, of course. But they liked the seclusion. There was something about being under the stars, away from the streetlights of NDN City, with plenty of beer, that made them appreciate life.

"How many soldiers we got left, dog?" Hoss asked.

Maddog checked the ice chest between them. "Two," he answered, and passed one to Hoss. Hoss popped the beer open and took a long, satisfying shot.

"What do you think," he said. "Beer run?"

"We'd better, before it gets too late."

"I'm down to get faded tonight," said Hoss. "No doubt about it. What about you, dog?"

"You ain't even got to ask," he answered. Then Maddog grabbed the last can of beer and said, "Let's get the fuck out of here, then."

As they made their way over to Hoss's car, Silver (a.k.a. the Car That Would Never Die), Maddog popped open his can of beer. Instead of hearing the usual *ssshhh* sound, a different sound came from the can. "You win!" it said.

"What the——?" exclaimed Maddog, thinking he was tripping from the weed.

"What the fuck was that?" Hoss asked. He and Maddog stopped and stared at the can. Then it hit them.

"Holy shit!" they said. Maddog pulled the tab again and again and again.

"You win!" "You win!" "You win!"

"It's the winning beer can!" Hoss blurted out. "From that commercial!"

"No fuckin' way," said Maddog.

"It's gotta be, dog."

"No. Somebody's gotta be fuckin' with us."

"Check it out, then. See what it says."

"Let me see. It says, *To claim your prize of one million dollars* . . . Oh, shit! I have to call this number on the can any time between eight a.m. and five p.m. Central time, Monday through Friday. It also says that I am subject to be video-recorded upon arrival of the check."

"Damn, dog. We're going to be fuckin' rich!"

"What? Wait, wait," Maddog said. He was confused. "What do you mean, 'we'?"

"Yeah, me and you. We'll split it fifty-fifty."

"Fifty-fifty? But this is my can."

"But I'm the one who bought it, so, technically, it's mine, too."

"No, no, no. You gave it to me, which, technically, makes it mine, all mine."

"Fuck that; I didn't give you shit. You're the one who grabbed the can from the ice chest. Remember? The ice chest of beer I was sharing with you, fifty-fifty. Come to think of it, you probably knew it was the winning can, so you handed me the other one."

"What? You trying to say I stole it from you? Fuck that. I ain't giving you shit now."

"Don't be playing, dog. This is some serious shit."

"Whatcha going to do?" asked Maddog, suddenly aggressive. It was a standoff: the bear versus the rabbit. Hoss was no match for Maddog, yet still he had no fear of him. Hoss clenched his fists. "Don't make me knock your punk ass out," said Maddog. "You're not gettin' this can, and that's fuckin' that." Maddog was in his battle stance. Hoss backed off, but there was anger in his eyes—almost hate.

"If you're going to be a bitch about it," he said, "you and your can can walk home."

"Fine with me. Fuckin' Indian giver."

Hoss stormed over to Silver and sped off, spewing a cloud of moonlit dust behind him. Maddog just stood there and watched, bewildered. They had had their fights in the past. Hoss had even threatened to leave him before but had never gone through with it, not like this. When Silver's taillights finally disappeared from view, Maddog thought it might just be the alcohol. Then he began his long walk home, holding his winning can of beer as though it were the firstborn son.

As he drove, Hoss went over and over the worth of the can in his head: one million dollars. The sum of the prize took him on an imaginary spending spree, where he paid all of Rose's bills, where he bought Li'l Hoss everything a boy could want, and where he purchased his own place. The money would surely grab Storm's attention. At that sudden revelation, Hoss made a decision to turn around and claim what was rightfully his, half of one million dollars. One way or another, he would get it.

Maddog was halfway down the road that went across the dam of the lake. His beer buzz had worn off, but he didn't care. He was daydreaming about all the hellified bitches he'd have on his *thookaloo* once he got the money, and of the '64 Chevy Impala he'd buy to take them around. He even thought about taking a vacation, maybe visit Brando in the White Man's Territory. Maddog was shaken out of his daydreams by headlights coming toward him from the other side of the dam. He recognized the headlights.

"That's my Native," Maddog whispered. He and Hoss were best friends. Nothing could come between them.

Hoss's anger grew with every ounce of gas he burned on his way back across the dam. Maddog had no business acting the way he had about the prize money. Hell, if it wasn't for Hoss, Maddog wouldn't even be getting anything. Shit was about to go down, for reals.

The headlights grew closer, and Maddog was cheering up. Not only would he get a ride back into NDN City, but he could still get his drink on. The night was young and now there was something to celebrate. The headlights were closer still. Maddog couldn't wait to tell Hoss all about his plans, plans that involved Hoss. They could get their business going again. They could take trips. Maddog wouldn't leave his best friend hanging. Maddog ran into the middle of the road and started waving his arms.

Hoss saw Maddog and began to slow down. And he began to prepare himself for the argument at hand. But as Silver came right up on Maddog, Hoss saw something that didn't sit too well with him. Actually, it offended him profoundly. Maddog was smiling. That stupid grin released a monster in Hoss. His best friend was rubbing it in, practically laughing at him. But this wasn't a joke. There was a million dollars at stake. A million dollars that should be all his, could be all his, if— Hoss never wasted time thinking about something before doing it. He struck first and faced consequences later. That was why he was in the situation he was with Rose and Storm. Now, with as little forethought and compassion, and with Maddog standing in the middle of the road, grinning from ear to ear, Hoss put the pedal to the metal. Silver's tires screamed in terror.

The television was on now, and, though Rose was staring right at it, she tuned out the Brewer's beer commercial announcing a contest. It was a commercial she had seen one too many times, anyway. Her focus was all on her anger, and it was getting the better of her. Evil and hateful thoughts raced through her mind. The only thing she could think about was the answer to her question. It was an answer that Hoss probably wouldn't be man enough to give her. Regardless, she was going to ask. Then she was going to kick his ass out. And so she sat and she waited some more.

Storm was just a little girl at her family's small, modest house in Apacheapolis. It was too nice to be inside, but she and her sister were playing in their living room nevertheless. They had a raggedy dollhouse and a few old Barbie dolls. Their alcohol-aged mother watched with a smile on her face that only her children could put there. There was a noise outside—their father was home! Like a gust of violent wind, he entered the house. He had been drinking all night. There was fear, no happiness.

"Why, you little whore!" he yelled at Storm's mother. "Did you think I wouldn't find out? Who was he? Who was he?" Storm's mother's eyes filled with fright as he went for her. She tried to get up but was met by a powerful blow to her jaw that thrust her back onto the couch. Storm and her sister grabbed each other, protected each other, and screamed at the top of their lungs. Irritated by their screams, their drunk father yelled, but Storm and her sister were screaming so loud that they couldn't hear his threats. He went after them next. When they saw him coming, Storm and her sister both took cover, just the way they were taught in tornado drills. Their father removed his belt.

Storm heard a loud crack, then felt pain. There was another crack. He struck her sister. Then he struck her again and her sister again. It burned and burned and burned.

Storm looked up just in time to see her sister reach for her Barbie doll and their father's belt buckle come crashing down on her sister's hand. A different crack was heard; bones broke. Storm knew their father had no intention of stopping, so she rose immediately to her sister's aid and jumped on top of her, shielding her from further blows. The belt buckle came down again, this time toward Storm's head. She could see it, and in slow motion she watched it coming. And just as it hit her . . .

Storm violently awakened, sweating and breathing hard. A single tear had made it halfway down her face. Instantly, there came comfort. She was glad it was only a dream and not the actual time it had happened. Her sister lost the use of three of her fingers that day. It was times like that Storm blamed for her problematic life. Those times had also driven her sister into the life she lived, as a coke-addicted stripper. And those times were why Storm was still struggling to make something of herself. She was the only one out of the two who had a chance. But as each day passed, it became less and less likely that she'd ever pull it off.

On his way back to NDN City, Hoss went over his alibi, just in case he needed one, just in case somebody happened to find the body of a large X-Indian man dumped down an old abandoned oil-well shaft. But murders were rarely solved in NDN City. In the passenger seat, where his best friend would normally ride, sat a beer can. Hoss picked it up and admired it. For kicks, he pulled the tab.

"You win!" said the beer can.

"Damn right I do," Hoss replied.

Rose had made a promise to herself to go to bed at three o'clock, but it was a promise she didn't need to keep. At 2:45 a.m., Hoss returned. Rose steeled herself for the argument that was about to walk in the door. She prayed for the strength to kick his ass out. The sound of his keys jangling at the lock sent a rush of adrenaline shooting through her body. The door swung open and Hoss barged in. Before she could say anything, Hoss slammed the door behind him, rushed right past Rose, as if she wasn't even there, and went straight to their bedroom. With an angry stride, Rose followed him in. But there she got a surprise. He was packing his shit.

"Where the hell are you going?" she asked.

"I'm fuckin' outta here," he answered, filling a gym bag with his clothes.

"What do you mean, you're fuckin' outta here?"

"We're through."

Rose was speechless. Somehow or other, he had turned the tables. Suddenly she wanted him to stay.

"Is there someone else?" she asked curtly.

"No. I'm just tired of your shit, that's all."

"Tired of my shit?"

"Listen, I don't want to do this right now, okay?"

"Who is she?" Rose demanded.

Storm lay in bed, listening to the conversation through the thin wall. Silently, she pleaded with Hoss not to say her name. That was the last thing she needed. She didn't have anywhere else to live. Her sister lived with some guys, her mother had kicked her out of her house, and no one else cared for her enough to take her in. There were few people she could rely on. Her cousin Rose may have been the only one. But that was now debatable.

Hoss ignored Rose. He had enough clothes to last a few days, so he zipped up the gym bag. Rose was not happy with the outcome. She was supposed to be the one in control, but she was being shunned. Rose raised her voice. "Who the fuck is she, Hoss?"

"Keep it down. Damn, you're going to wake up Li'l Hoss."

"Don't you act worried about him! Anyways, he's at my mom's! Now tell me, fucker! Who is she?" Rose never cursed. There was rage behind the word she chose; there was hurt in her voice; there were years and years of looking the other way. Hoss knew he wasn't going to get out of it too easy.

"What do you wanna hear?" he threw at her. "You wanna hear how I can't stop fucking other women, how I'll fuck the first piece of pussy that gives me a second glance? How I've been getting blow jobs from some chicks up in Bethlehem?"

Rose was silenced. His words cut her deep. And in that moment, love crossed over that thin line into hate.

"I hate you. I fuckin' hate you!" she sobbed, then lunged at Hoss and clawed his face with her nails.

"Oh, you fuckin' bitch!" Hoss yelled. He felt the blood on his face, and the monster in him was released again. He backhanded Rose. She hit the wall but sprang back quickly. She lunged at him again, this time landing on his back. She grabbed him by the neck and, before Hoss could react, bit into his flesh.

"AAAHHH!" he screamed. He reached back, grabbed Rose by the hair, and pulled as hard as he could. It took a few hard tugs, but he managed to get her off him. Then he swung her by her hair and threw her across the room. She hit the wall so hard, it dazed her. She saw it coming—the monster. And before she could cry out for help, the monster attacked.

Hoss had just bought himself some more time, so he packed another bag, enough so that he would never have to return. There were items stored away in their closet that he wanted: pictures, his hats, and baseball cards. He packed them all inside a backpack, then stashed the winning beer can in there, too. He was leaving NDN City and was contemplating waking Storm. He had always wanted to whisk someone away in the middle of the night. It would have been very romantic, very Scarface-ish.

Rose wasn't dead, nor was she unconscious; she just couldn't move. Her eyes were almost swollen shut; her lips were too swollen to speak. She watched Hoss—the father of her child, the love of her life, the man who had just gotten through beating her—preparing to leave her. And still she wanted to know who the girl was.

When Hoss had taken all he wanted from his life with Rose, he opened the bedroom door to leave and was surprised to see Storm standing there. He smiled.

In her delicate hands was the baseball bat that Hoss kept in the living-room closet. Storm swung her hardest. There was a loud crack of bones fracturing. Hoss was on the ground when Storm delivered the second blow. And the third, and the fourth, and the fifth. . . .

It hurt Rose to move, but she and Storm had to do something with Hoss's body—before Li'l Hoss got home, before anyone came by, before the sun rose. Storm knew of a place: an old abandoned oil-well site that Hoss had actually taken her to on several occasions. Of course, she didn't tell Rose that, but she did find it ironic.

Somehow, Rose and Storm managed to carry Hoss's lifeless body all the way out to Silver. They got him into the trunk of his own car, along with all of his belongings.

In half an hour, they were at the old abandoned oil-well site, dragging Hoss's body to a shaft in the ground, an opening just big enough for a body. Without any condolences offered, Hoss went headfirst down the shaft. A few seconds of silence, then a soft thud was heard. The shaft had to be at least fifty feet deep. Rose and Storm tossed all of his belongings down after him. After his backpack hit the bottom, they both could have sworn that they heard a ghost whisper, "You win!"

You Better Recognize
2001

Twenty-four-year-old Marlon Buffalo was on his usual Friday lunch break.

Every Friday he would eat at a new restaurant—one he hadn't tried before—in the downtown area of Columbus City. He had been living there for a while now and was even proud to call it his home. It hadn't always been his home, though; his real home was the drug-driven, X-Indian–populated NDN City. A place he had barely managed to escape. How he managed to escape—well, that was a whole different story. There was a be-trayal, not to mention all them damn cops. But that was all in the past, thanks to the statute of limitations.

Though he didn't work out all that much anymore, he was still toned and still as tall as ever, but he no longer wore his hair long and back in a ponytail. Now he had short hair. And there was a civilized way about him; he was no longer rough around the edges. People had to look twice to see that he was an X-Indian, he dressed that good. His suits were designer made, top-of-the-line. They hid his dark skin.

After lunch at the fine Greek restaurant he had chosen, it was time for Marlon to return to his job as a lawyer at the Courtroom of Humanity. It was the first job he had landed after graduating from the University of the White Man's Ways. It paid well, but the highest-paying job Marlon had ever had was the only other job he had ever had, back in NDN City. He'd been a drug dealer. In fact, he'd been the leader of a small drug cartel.

Now it was a whole different story. He did things right. And his wife, Two-Rivers-Flowing-Together, was extremely proud of him for that. He had a legit job, a traceable income, and credit! She couldn't have been happier, and if there was one thing Marlon loved, it was making her happy, making their children happy. He had a blissful new life, far away from NDN City.

Marlon left a good tip and started back toward work. As he walked, he thought about the weekend. Maybe they could go to the lake. Or a movie? So many possibilities. But there came an interruption, unexpected physical contact. Marlon was shoved from behind. He lurched and almost lost his balance.

"What up, fool?" came a young man's voice from behind him.

Marlon whirled around, ready to defend himself, but was greeted by a tall, skinny, smiling X-Indian, or maybe he was Mexican. Had to be X-Indian. The way he braided his long X-Indian hair gave that away. The stranger looked vaguely familiar to Marlon. He searched his mind for a name to fit the glossy face, but the strong scent of beer coming from the stranger distracted him. Then, for some reason or other, Marlon got the impression that the stranger might be from NDN City. He had to be, by the way he was dressed: plain white T-shirt, baggy denim shorts, sandals, and a black hat—the uniform of most X-Indians from around that way. The stranger couldn't have been a day older than sixteen. Maybe he was one of the dozen or so kids that used to run around NDN City worshipping Marlon back in the day. Marlon had heard they all grew up fast.

"Don't tell me you don't know a Native?" said the stranger jovially.

In his old 'hood, a person could get beat down for forgetting a homeboy's name. Not that Marlon was scared of the stranger; it was just the code. "Hey, what's up?" he said.

"Just chillin' in this lame-ass white-boy bar. You know how I do it."

"You ain't twenty-one, are you?" Marlon asked, only because he didn't look it.

"Shit, I wish. Fake ID, fool. Fake ID. Damn, look at your ass, all decked out in a suit and tie. Who died? And . . . Oh, shit! You cut your hair?"

"Yeah, it's been short for a minute now; got tired of that chief look. So, how long has it been?" Marlon asked, hoping for a clue that would help him remember the stranger.

"Since that one night, when we did acid together. Remember?"

Marlon recalled nights like that in a dozen different ways, so the stranger could've been anybody. "That long, huh? Crazy. So, what brings you here? Going to school or what?"

"School? Fuck that. I'm just here to make a little money."

"You ballin' around here?"

"Nah, I had to bring a shipment up here for ole Jabba's ass. Anyways, I heard you was livin' up here, and I wanted to try and find your ass. Looks like I lucked off."

"Yeah. . . . Well, it was nice seeing you again. Take care," Marlon said, and tried to walk away. He didn't really want to find out who the stranger was.

"'Take care'? I know you just didn't. Fuck work; let's go get fucked up. Especially after I brought my ass all the way up here to kick it with you," the stranger said. "My treat."

Marlon stopped. "It's not even one o'clock in the afternoon," he said. "I'll tell you what, maybe we can get some drinks after I get off work. How's that?"

"You know, I saw this titty bar down the road. We could go check that out, man."

"Sounds like fun, but I'm married now," Marlon said, though it was tempting.

"What Two-Rivers don't know can't hurt her. Come on. Shit, don't make me beg. Oh, and I got some killer, too. We can get high as fuck, just like old times."

"I would, but I really do need to get back to work. Next time, for sure, *piah-phee*."

"But what if there ain't a next time, *piah-phee*?" said the stranger. "You never know."

"What do you mean?" Marlon asked.

"It's just . . . oh, never mind all that. What do you say? It's half a day. I know your punk ass can afford that with your big-time job."

"Actually, I wish I could, but they got me working on my first big case right now, so I'm piled up with work. I can't even afford to take an hour off."

"All right, all right. I'm not trying to fuck your shit all up, but can you at least do this one thing for me, Brando? Kind of like a favor?"

"What kind of favor?" Marlon asked, glad to see that their conversation was finally nearing an end. Marlon knew now that the stranger had to be from NDN City. Only people from NDN City knew him as Brando, the street name he earned from being just the slickest mutha-fucker ever.

"Hook me up with a ride back to NDN City."

"NDN City? Are you fuckin' crazy? That's over a twelve-hour drive from here." The nerve of him!

"Come on, it'll be the bomb, man. You could visit the tombstones they got for Hoss and Maddog, maybe even pay a visit to Morning-Dew. She still talks about you."

"As much as I almost want to, I really can't. Now, if you don't mind, I have to get back to work."

"Man, whatcha scared of? They're not looking for you anymore. Those warrants are too old."

"I'm not scared. I just don't want to go. But if you really need help getting back, I can give you a ride to the bus station," Marlon offered, "and buy you a ticket back home. How's that?"

"Bus station? Fuck that. Okay, I ain't going to bullshit you. I just wanna kick it with you, that's all."

"Like I said, maybe next time. I gotta get going," Marlon said for the last time, turning and walking away.

"You must really like sucking on the white man's dick," the stranger said to Marlon's back.

Marlon stopped and turned.

"Excuse me?"

"You heard me. What? What are you going to do? Sue me?"

"Listen here, boy. I was just trying to be polite, but if you want to act like this, fuck you."

"I guess it is true, what everybody's been saying about you down there."

"Oh, yeah, and what's that?" Marlon asked. This he had to hear.

"You're a sellout."

"Let me fill you in on something, boy. I ran the streets in NDN City when you were probably nothing more than a snot-nosed brat, which looks like it hasn't changed much. And if there was ever anybody down for his shit, it was me, muthafucker. I did my time in that hellhole, and then I got the fuck out."

"You left, just like a sellout would."

"Maybe, but so what? Like I give a fuck what you or them little punks down there have to say about me. You better just take your ass on, boy."

"Or what?" asked the stranger. There were now a few onlookers. Arguments between people of color were not common in that area. Marlon decided to be the better man and end the confrontation. He turned and walked away once more.

Marlon almost expected it, so it should not have been a surprise when the stranger spun him around and punched him dead in the jaw. Marlon's legs gave out, and he hit the sidewalk with all of his weight. It hurt. When he tried to get up, he was driven back down by a series of piercing kicks from the stranger. Marlon did what any other man would have done—he curled up into a ball, just like the armadillo had taught his people to do. It worked. His back would end up with a few bruises, but life would go on. The stranger, realizing that he was inflicting little damage, stopped kicking Marlon. But it wasn't over.

"You better recognize, bitch!" he yelled. "Look at you, lying there all curled up like a baby. Get up!" More onlookers had gathered.

"Police!" Marlon shouted at them. "Someone call the police!" If he'd really wanted to, he could have gotten up and fought the stranger off himself, but it just wasn't in him anymore. It had been that long since he'd been in a fight. Violence had a different effect on him than before. Now he was actually afraid of it.

"Here, I'll help," said the stranger. "Police! Can somebody call the police to help this bitch-ass trick?"

"I'm warning you," said Marlon. "You better get outta here while you can. They don't put up with punks like you here."

"Did you forget who the hell you're talkin' to?" said the stranger. "I ain't scared of no police." And he pulled a shiny gun from his pocket. The onlookers scattered and took cover wherever they could. Marlon was terrified. He pulled out his wallet and threw it at the stranger, who was unusually calm, and entertained by the effect he had.

"Here, take it all," Marlon screamed like a bitch. "Just don't shoot me!"

"I don't want your fuckin' money. All I wanted was to kick it with you. But, no, you had to be an asshole about it. Now look at you, man. Can't even hold your own ground. It's fuckin' pathetic. And what's even more fucked up, I bet you don't even know who I am, do you? And to think I missed your ass." The fact that the police were probably on their way didn't seem to bother the stranger at all.

"What?"

"I felt it, man. You were missing me, too. That's why I came to see your punk ass. But apparently you don't know me, and I definitely don't know you anymore. Well, Mr. Law and Order, this was our last chance, and you fuckin' blew it. Laterz." The stranger was actually trying to hold back tears. He put his gun back into his pocket and rushed away.

Embarrassed, Marlon got up from the ground and wiped the dust off his arms. He tried to make sense of the little encounter, tried desperately to remember who the stranger was. Then it dawned on him! The stranger wasn't a stranger at all; far from it. The stranger was *him*. The stranger was Marlon in his younger years, before he got an education, before he moved out of the 'hood, and before he gave a damn about anything!

It all made sense. In his younger years, it was his thing to start drinking early in the day, and he was never without some good chronic. And the gun—he should have recognized that right off the bat. It was his favorite piece, a nickel-plated .45.

"How could I have missed it?" Marlon wondered. Then the reason hit him, in the jaw, as the stranger had. Marlon had changed that much, so much that he couldn't even recognize who he used to be. Whether that was good or bad, he didn't know. Maybe he *was* a sellout?

Memories flared in Marlon's mind. He remembered how crazy and careless he used to be, how much fun it was, how he never gave a fuck about anything, how he feared nothing. A smile spread over his face, a smile he hadn't smiled in a long time. There was a hint of wickedness in it. Maybe catching up on old times wasn't such a bad idea. Fuck work!

Marlon jogged off in the direction of the stranger, still visible at the end of the block. The stranger then turned a corner, and Marlon broke into a harder stride. When Marlon reached the corner, to his surprise there was no one there. The street was empty, as if the younger Marlon had just vanished.

Was Marlon going crazy? Did he imagine the whole thing? Would the cops believe his story? At that thought, he knew better than to stand around and wait for them. He returned to work, the sound of sirens fading behind him. Marlon didn't know what exactly had gone down, but he did know this: he would never see him again.

Grandma Blessing
2002

It had been six years since Mausape was relocated to the northern part of the Indian Territory, near the Great Lakes, and he still wasn't used to the harsh winters. It made the drive home, to his little house in the middle of nowhere, uncertain at times.

Mausape didn't normally light up, but on this night, there were enough reasons for him to do so, and the cab of his truck was filled with cigarette smoke. The main reason for a smoke right then was that he was more nervous than he had ever been in his life. His nervousness didn't sit too well with his stomach, either. He reached for a half-empty bottle of Pepto-Bismol and took a swig. Then he took another puff of his menthol cigarette and continued the journey home to confront his wife, Desire.

Desire had been his wife for eight years now, and he still defined beauty as just one look at her. Yet her beauty was only one of the many things that pleased him about her. There was also the fact that she loved him unconditionally. Who else would have relocated with him as part of the Witness Protection Program after he betrayed his best friend some six years earlier? She was the only one there for him, the only one who wanted to help him start over. She had always been loyal and faithful to Mausape. That is, until lately.

Since Mausape had settled into his new home with his lovely wife, he had started to write his first book. It had always been his goal to be a writer. As most writers did, he wrote what he knew. He wrote about what it was like to be an X Indian; he wrote about the trials and tribulations of being an X-Indian; he wrote stories involving his X-Indian friends. Chapter after chapter, story after story, he wrote for six years. It kept him unemployed, turned him antisocial, and used up a lot of time he should have spent with Desire. She was always lonely because of that damn book. Mausape's obsession with his book literally drove her away. Whenever he started to write, she left, sometimes for days at a time. The worst thing about it was that Mausape never even noticed. That is, until lately.

Mausape had just finished the last chapter of his book and decided to celebrate with his wife, his one love. Eagerly, he had shot out of his study and to the bedroom to wake her. He flicked on the light, expecting to see

Desire buried under blankets. Instead, he had found their bedroom empty. Not only that, but the bed looked as if no one had slept in it for quite some time.

Desire's absence triggered an army of questions. Where was she? How long had she been gone? When was the last time he saw her? He couldn't remember. He had slept in his study all week, trying to finish up his book. But he had recollected one thing—a couple of days earlier, she had asked him to a movie or something, but he had declined her invitation. Maybe she had left him again. Or maybe she had been kidnapped or abducted by aliens.

The ridiculous questions could be answered more easily, so he had started with them. To verify that there hadn't been a kidnapping, he turned their home upside down searching for clues of a struggle. It was while he was digging through their dirty laundry that he had made a discovery. A note fell out from a pocket of her jeans. It was a poem, handwritten.

SAP
I often find myself enjoying your sweet sap,
the taste, the effect,
while you blossom with the most beautiful sounds.
I pollinate your soul
and you grow more in love with me,
while rain emerges from you, by me.

I cause the fruits of your bosom to ripen,
photosynthesis occurs in your movements
and the sun is my tongue.

— *Sean Arrows*

By the time he had finished reading the poem, Mausape's eyes were watering. An earthquake of betrayal broke his heart, and his world came crumbling down. Desire was having an affair! Not only that, but Mausape knew the guy. Sean Arrows was Mausape's idol, the very person who inspired him to write, the god of all X-Indian writers, and a well published one, too. He had countless award-winning books under his belt.

Mausape had never actually met Sean Arrows, so how his wife had was baffling. That was soon to change, though; they would meet, just as Mausape had always dreamed, but under circumstances very different from what he had ever imagined.

Heartbroken, Mausape had fallen to the floor and wept. Over and over, he imagined his wife under another man. Image by image, tear by tear, Mausape cried away their love until there was nothing left inside his shattered heart. And he mourned no more.

Hate moved in to heal the wounds, and hate, as everyone knows, can give birth to death.

Mausape had then made a few phone calls, and by the

time the sun was almost halfway through the sky, he had discovered where Sean Arrows lived. As luck would have it, it wasn't too far—only forty-five minutes away. Mausape loaded up his truck with a few burying tools and grabbed his nine-millimeter pistol, then sped off toward Oneida Falls.

It was evening by the time Mausape found 401 East Colorado. The first thing he had noticed was that Desire's car wasn't there. Still, he pulled slowly into the short driveway of a large two-story house. There was a *Leave It to Beaver* quality to the neighborhood; every house there looked the same. It had made Mausape uneasy. If anything out of the ordinary happened in such a neighborhood, the neighbors would surely take notice. Mausape would have to move fast. He parked, then slid his gun into his pants. He couldn't believe he was about to do what his main character had done in the last chapter of his book: murder two adulterous people. Art imitating life, life imitating art. Either way, two fornicating muthafuckers were about to be gunned down, just like in his book.

Instead of going to the front door, he went straight around to the back. There he saw a pool, a guesthouse, and a bunch of ugly plants. The back door was unlocked.

Once he went inside, there was no turning back. Mausape pulled out his gun and clicked off the safety. He entered the kitchen. It was noticeably clean, too clean to be the kitchen of a single man. Mausape moved to leave the kitchen, but then something had caught his eye. On the counter next to the stove lay a pack of Marlboro Lights. That was Desire's brand of cigarettes, and she was never without them. She was a regular locomotive. The way she smoked, no one would ever believe that she had once been an angel. He picked up the pack, and, unsurprisingly, it was empty.

The cigarettes, the clean kitchen—it was too much for him. They had to die. He could already see their blood on the walls.

Mausape regained a little of his composure, then went on. He came to a closed door, then stopped to listen. From the other side of the door came a familiar sound, the sound of someone typing, someone writing. That someone had to be Mausape's greatest adversary. Beyond that door, a bloodbath awaited. The hate inside Mausape built until, in a rage, he kicked open the door. Blinded by his hate, he started shooting. Three times his gun went off, shooting the only person in the room. Sean Arrows had been sitting at his dining-room table, working on a laptop, when the bullets went through his chest.

"Where's Desire?" Mausape demanded, but Mr. Arrows died quick and silently. The screen of his laptop displaying the very last words the famous author would ever write: *He came to a closed door, then stopped to listen. From the other side of the door came a familiar sound, the sound of someone typing, someone writing. That someone had to be his greatest adversary. Beyond that door, a bloodbath awaited. The hate inside him built until, in a rage, he kicked open the door. . . .*

It had been six years since Mausape was relocated to the northern part of the Indian Territory, near the Great Lakes, and he still wasn't used to the harsh winters. It made the drive home, to his little house in the middle of nowhere, uncertain at times.

Mausape didn't normally light up, but on this night, there were enough reasons for him to do so, and the cab of his truck was filled with cigarette smoke. The main reason for a smoke right then was that he was more nervous than he had ever been in his life. His nervousness didn't sit too well with his stomach, either. He reached for a half-empty bottle of Pepto-Bismol and took a swig. Then he took another puff of his menthol cigarette and continued the journey home to confront his wife, Desire.

Mausape was driving down an old back road, far from any houses, when he saw something very peculiar. He passed an old lady walking along the side of the road. It was dark, and now it was snowing, and the old lady had on nothing but a thin dress.

It was cold, too cold to be walking. Mausape made a U-turn and pulled up alongside her.

The old lady was walking with her head buried in her chest, so she must not have seen Mausape rolling down his window or heard him ask if she wanted a ride. Or maybe she was just frightened. Whatever the reason, Mausape wasn't about to let her walk. He jumped out of the cab of his truck to get her attention.

"Hey, miss! Need a ride?" he yelled politely. "I can give you a ride to wherever you're going!" The old lady stopped and turned. "Thank you, son," she said kindly. Mausape could barely make out her face. It was the face of an old Indian woman, with wrinkles as old as Mausape. Her hair was salt-and-pepper and was pulled back in some kind of fancy braid. Mausape opened his passenger door and then remembered something of great importance. There was a dead man in the back of his truck. With a coating of snow now covering everything, though, he figured she probably wouldn't even notice. Mausape helped her into the cab of the truck. As she climbed in, Mausape took note of details. Her dress was dark red, with small yellow flowers sprinkled all over it—a very simple pattern. It was homemade and old-fashioned.

As soon as Mausape was back behind the wheel of his truck, he turned around and drove off into the cold, desolate night. Not too far down the road, he finally asked the old lady where she was headed, but she must have been too busy digging through a small buckskin bag to hear him. He continued driving home in silence. It was about five miles later that the old lady decided to speak.

"I really appreciate the ride. No telling what would've

happened to me out there. It's so cold." Her voice was slow and soft, like his grandma's.

"No problem. It can get a little dangerous out here at night, too. I've heard some bad stuff about this road."

"That's just a bunch of superstition. I grew up walking this road."

"Kids. I mean teenagers. They like to drink and drive around this way. They've been known to hit people."

"If I was meant to get hit, they would've hit me a long time ago." She laughed. Mausape smiled, not knowing what to say. "It's okay, son," she said. "A lot of people tell me the same thing."

"So, where were you coming from?"

"Oh, home."

"You must have somewhere pretty important to go to be walking in this weather."

"Just to town. My son got himself thrown in jail again, so I have to go bail him out. He's just like his daddy—always in bars or behind them." She laughed again.

"I hate to tell you this," Mausape said, "but town is in the opposite direction."

"It is? I didn't know. . . . This weather, it always confuses me."

"I'll tell you what: I'm in no hurry to get home. I'll take you to town real quick."

"No, I don't want to be a burden on you. Really, I can walk."

"No, I'd be happy to. It would be my good deed for the day. Really."

"Well, I sure do appreciate it, son. Can never have too many good deeds. Not in these troubling times," she said, but there was something in the way she said it that made Mausape uneasy.

"Don't mention it."

Mausape and the old lady drifted back into silence as he made another U-turn and drove back toward town, a good fifteen minutes away. The old lady smelled kind of the way his grandmother used to smell. Maybe it was the smell of age. It wasn't a bad smell. It was just a smell that brought back memories of his home and his family, neither of which he had seen since he'd been relocated six years earlier. He wondered if his grandma was still alive. He'd probably never know, because by the time the night was over, there were only two places he could end up: jail or hell. And he preferred the latter.

"Your grandma's alive and doing well," the old lady said, breaking the silence.

"What? How did you . . . ?"

"How did I know you were thinking about her? I've got my ways, son."

"Are you like a medicine woman or something?"

"I wouldn't say that."

"Psychic?"

"Oh, no. Reading minds is for the carnival folk. I do use medicine, though. And my medicine told me to tell you that your grandma is well. My medicine never lies, son. Do you believe in medicine?"

"I don't know, a little bit. My grandma used to use her medicine when somebody in our family got sick, and it always made them better."

"Yes, she had good medicine. I have good medicine, too."

"Is there such a thing as bad medicine?"

"Sure there is. Even in medicine there is a battle between good and evil."

Silence filled the cab of the truck once again.

"Do you want to talk about it?" the old lady asked out of the blue.

"Talk about what?"

"Your loved one."

"Loved one?" Mausape replied, hoping she didn't sense the evil there.

"Yes. Aren't you on your way to your loved one?" asked the old lady.

"I don't know if I'd call her a loved one anymore."

"I sense trouble."

Mausape felt that uneasiness in his stomach again. She might be on to him. Her medicine might have told her.

But in case that wasn't so, he decided to share some of his situation with her.

"Actually, there has been a little trouble."

"With her or with you?"

"Her, my loved one, my wife. I found out that she's been cheating on me."

"I'm sorry to hear that, son. But the women of today, they don't seem to know their place. Back in my day, if a wife ever got caught cheating on her husband, he would have the right to cut off her nose and that was considered their divorce. After that, she could marry whomever she pleased. That is, if she could find anyone who wanted to marry her."

"Well, if they still did that, there would be a lot of noseless women out there today."

"Ain't that the truth," the old lady said, and then they both laughed, a well-deserved laugh. "So what do you think made her do such a terrible thing?"

"What do you mean? Do you mean, did I have something to do with it?"

"No, I'm just curious. What makes the women of today do such things?"

"I don't know. I might have had a little to do with it. You see, I'm a writer and I've been spending a lot of time writing this book."

"A storyteller, huh?"

"Yeah, you could say that."

"And she left you because of your storytelling?"

"Yeah."

"Well, if there's one thing I've learned about story-tellers," she said, "it's that they can always start a new story." She was right there, and it was exactly what Mausape needed to hear. He could almost hug the old lady.

"Yeah, but I have to end the old story first."

"There's nothing like a good ending."

A chill ran up Mausape's spine. He turned to say something else, but the old lady was gone. She was no longer in his truck, no longer sitting there beside him. She had vanished. Mausape slammed on the brakes, nearly sliding into a ditch. He looked all over for her—inside his truck, outside his truck, even in the truck bed. There was no sign of the old lady. But in the place where she'd been sitting, she left something, a sign that proved he wasn't going crazy or that he had imagined the whole encounter. It was a small pouch made out of buckskin. He picked it up carefully and looked it over. It was a medicine pouch, maybe a gift.

Mausape wondered what was inside, but he knew that a medicine pouch was never supposed to be opened. Its blessing could easily become a curse. Some said bones were inside, some said flesh, but they were probably just filled with something innocent, like the root of a common plant or a few pebbles. Whatever it contained, whatever power it possessed, it was his. He placed the pouch in his pocket and remembered that he had a body in his truck and that he was on his way to kill his wife. First things first, so he gave up his search for the old woman and left.

Nearly a pack of cigarettes later, Mausape pulled into his driveway. It was at the end of a short dirt road that went through a small field and a thicket of trees. If ever there was a perfect place to kill somebody, his house was it. Their nearest neighbor was three miles down the road.

Mausape pulled up in the usual manner, got out of his truck, and was greeted by the smells of his wife cooking supper. Chicken and fried potatoes. The aroma was enough to make him postpone his deed until after he ate. It would be their very own Last Supper. He felt surprisingly calm as he walked into the house and saw her. She looked more beautiful to him in that moment than she had ever looked to him, almost angelic again.

She greeted him with a smile. "There you are."

"Just in time," he said. Mausape would play the innocent game, too.

"Where were you?" she asked. Before answering, he walked past her, went into the living room, made himself comfortable on the couch, picked up the remote, and turned on the television.

Finally he answered, "Went to town to get some things I needed."

"Supper's just about done."

"Good, I'm starving. How was your day?"

"All right, I guess. Went to Oneida Falls earlier, did some shopping. That's about it."

"What'd you get?" he asked.

"Um, just some stuff for the house. How are the roads out there?" she asked, changing the subject. "The snow cover them up yet?" Mausape was amused.

"Almost. Why? Got somewhere to go?"

"No. I was just wondering."

Their conversation was fake; nothing was being said. Mausape then recalled the encounter he had had with the old lady. Maybe talking about that would make better conversation and help them pass the time while they ate, before she died. His wife loved ghost stories.

"Something strange happened to me on the way home tonight," he began.

"What?"

"I saw this old lady walking on the side of the road in the middle of nowhere. And it was all snowing and shit. Can you believe, she only had this thin dress thing on?"

"Did you pick her up?"

"Yeah, she said she was going to town. But that's another thing—she was walking the wrong way. Anyways, I told her I'd take her back to town, and the whole way, we were talking and stuff. Then when we were pretty close to town, I looked over and she was gone, just disappeared into thin air. I couldn't find her anywhere. I even drove back to see if she had fallen out of the truck or something, but I didn't find anything."

"Oh, my God. You picked up Grandma Blessing!"

"Who?"

"Grandma Blessing. The people talk about her all the time around here."

"Grandma Blessing? What is she, some kind of ghost?"

"Something like that. But a good ghost. They say that she froze to death a long time ago while walking to town."

"To get her son out of jail?"

"I don't know, but they say now she walks the road lost—just back and forth—all the time. And they say that if you pick her up and give her a ride that she'll give you a blessing, something good will happen to you. So, looks like something good's going to happen to you, Mausape." Desire finished frying the last piece of chicken. She turned off the stove and began to set the table.

Mausape felt his pocket. The medicine pouch was still there. He decided to leave out that part of the story. It wasn't important. What was important was that his love for Desire had died, and he was suddenly anxious to send her back to the heaven she came from. His need to kill her was coming on so strong—why, he didn't know—but he was done with the innocent game. He would eat later.

"Speaking of something good happening, I got you a little present."

"A present?" she asked in disbelief. "What for?"

"I don't know. I guess for putting up with me."

"Now, I do deserve something for that. Where's it at?"

"Outside, in the truck. We'll have to go outside to see it."

"You can't bring it in?"

"It's too big. Come on, I'll show you." His wife was gleaming with excitement as Mausape led her outside to her death. His heart was pounding out of control, its first sign of life since being broken. He had once believed that she was his soul mate, but now it hit him: how could that be when she didn't even have a soul? She was an angel turned mortal. It was all a scam and he'd been taken. But it would be over soon. They were standing at the back of his truck now. A streetlamp provided what little light they needed.

"I kind of want it to be a surprise," Mausape told Desire, "so close your eyes." She closed her eyes. Mausape opened the tailgate. The sight of the carcass did something to him. It brought him back to reality. His heart pounded out of control. His mouth got very, very dry. He started to feel panicky and dizzy.

"Come on, it's cold out here," he heard his wife say. "Can I open my eyes?" He couldn't even answer.

He grew even more dizzy, felt like he might throw up. Anxiety overcame him. He thought about backing out and running away, but that was no longer an option. He'd gone too far already. Mausape grabbed his gun.

"All right, I'm opening my eyes," she said, a mixture of curiosity and fear in her voice. She opened her eyes, only to see a gun. There was a rush of wind and the loudest ringing noise she had ever heard, then blackness.

When Mausape pulled the trigger, the bullet went right between his wife's eyes. It was the biggest surprise of her life. Blood flew everywhere. And Mausape watched her take her last breath. He watched her twitch involuntarily on the cold ground. He watched her soulless body die.

His wife's body lying lifeless in the snow and Mr. Arrows's body in the bed of his truck, Mausape went back inside and ate dinner. (Chicken and fried potatoes. Delicious.) It was official: Mausape had lost his mind.

As Mausape ate, he thought about the ending of this story. It lacked something; it needed something more. (Desire's chicken had never tasted so good.) Ideas floated in and out of his head, like they normally did, but none were worthy. Killing himself was an obvious conclusion, but it didn't appeal to him: too easy. Mausape's stories were always cutting-edge. Finally, he hit on the right idea. He pulled the medicine pouch from his pocket. If the stories were true, if Grandma Blessing was real, then the medicine pouch was the key to the perfect ending.

Mausape held the pouch between his hands and prayed with all of his mental might, not to the Great Spirit, but to Grandma Blessing. He prayed to her and he pleaded with her. Then something happened. The medicine pouch exploded in his hands. The contents flew into the air, then came raining down onto Mausape. It was an odd-colored powder and smelled awful.

Mausape started to cough, then he began to choke, unable to breathe. He grabbed his chest, but something far from obvious had happened—his chest was gone. Mausape looked down and saw only emptiness. He reached for his chest again to discover that his hands were gone, too. They had vanished from his arms. Mausape screamed as he watched the rest of his body disappear. There was no blood left, nothing; just an empty void where his body should have been. It was the powder. Wherever the powder landed on Mausape, he was dissolved into nothing. Mausape was confused. Either he was getting his perfect ending or the Great Spirit was playing a sick joke on him. Either way, the end was near.

When there was nothing of Mausape left but his thoughts, a terrible wind came rushing through his house. It blew Mausape right out the kitchen door, past his truck, and up into the night sky. Mausape watched his house shrink into the distance until it was no more than a dot, and then nothing.

It took him a while, but once Mausape got used to it, he found that gliding through the air as wind was soothing, liberating. And as he blew through the night sky, he wondered, Had his wish come true? Had he, indeed, become a story? Or a wind? Either was more preferable than life.

For days he drifted high above the clouds, over town after town, city after city, until one night he began to lose altitude. Faster and faster, he plummeted toward a city he recognized right away. It was the place where his story began. It was the last place he wanted it to end! But against his will, he was blown toward NDN City and a neighborhood he knew well: Bethlehem, where he grew up. But he was approaching a house he didn't recognize.

Mausape was pulled toward an open window in the back of the unfamiliar house. Through the window, he could see a young X-Indian man seated at a desk, a notebook in front of him, a pencil in his hand. It was then that Mausape finally realized what he truly was. He was neither man nor wind nor story; he was an idea, a story in its infancy. Mausape blew into the room, and landed right on the mind of the writer. And in that moment, Thomas M. Yeahpau began to write. He wrote the perfect ending to a perfect story.

And so Mausape became this story, this book, and exists only here, on these pages that Thomas M. Yeahpau has written just for you.

X-Indian Dayz

The dayz are gone
The dayz are gone

Our people are left short
for the dayz we long
for the dayz we long

Only a memory are
the dayz we roamed
the dayz we roamed

But we still dance
to our dayz last song
to our dayz last song

And even though we sing
dayz come home
dayz come home

The dayz stay gone
The dayz stay gone